Murder Most Fowl

The Gumboot & Gumshoe Series: Book Three

Laura Hesse

Running L Productions

ISBN-13 (print): 978-1999077402

National Library of Canada Cataloguing in Publication Data
Hesse, Laura - 1959 Murder Most Fowl/by Laura Hesse

Cover Artist: Autumn Sky, Self Pub Book Covers Inc.

Publisher: Running L. Productions, Vancouver Island, British Columbia, Canada

Introduction

Gumboots, Gumshoes and Murder is the first book in The Gumboot and Gumshoe Series followed by The Dastardly Mr. Deeds, Murder Most Fowl, and the standalone story, Gertrude & The Sorcerer's Gold.

While the first two novels in the series were inspired by actual events in British Columbia and in the U.S. coupled with copious amounts of wine and a few bizarre stories shared by a friend, Murder Most Fowl isn't inspired by anything except my warped imagination and a love of black comedies.

Gertrude, the pot-bellied pig, is based on Alfie, a wonderful fellow who would do anything for a Milk Bone.

Seal Island is loosely based on Lasqueti Island, a wonderful piece of paradise located between Vancouver Island and the mainland of British Columbia. It is only accessible by ferry, boat or sea plane.

Contents

Prelude

Betty flew out of the bed. She quickly slipped a sweater over top of her pyjama top and a pair of blue jeans. She snatched up her cell phone and Summer River's ragged diary before racing down the stairs.

Outside, the sun was setting behind Watchtower Mountain. Stars were beginning to sparkle over head. Creeping shadows danced among the evergreens that lined the driveway.

Betty felt chilled to the bone, despite the downy jacket and hiking boots she had slipped on before heading down to the Bristling Boar Pub.

Vi had no idea how much danger she was is, and neither did Betty's father for that matter.

Betty increased her pace as she bolted down the hill, heading towards the landing. It got darker and darker as she ran down the gravel road until there was only starlight coupled with the muted glow from solar lanterns lining the odd driveway to light her way.

How on earth was she going to tell her father she suspected his best friend of murder?

She tugged out her phone and breathlessly called Inspector Tom Powder, the lead investigator into the bizarre deaths of Summer River, Eliza Bone and Tiffany Hyde-White.

She slowed her pace briefly as her call to the Inspector went to voice mail.

"Tom, it's Betty," she huffed, breathless from her run. "I've been reading Summer's diary. I think I know who the father is. Call me as soon as you can."

Betty ended the call and increased her pace once again. Her knees screamed from the beating they were taking. Her heart pounded against her rib cage. Sweat poured down her face and soaked her flannel PJ top beneath her sweater and coat. At fifty-two, she hadn't expected to be running a marathon, but she was glad she had kept up with her training, despite retiring from the force a few days ago.

***

At the same time that Betty was racing towards the pub, the beginning of North Shore Road, a hippie girl with flowing skirts, brightly colored gumboots, dread locked hair, and a homespun coat of many colors was racing towards Betty's house from her farm at the far end of North Shore Road. Her two dogs galloped along beside her.

Terror fueled Rainbow McDonald. She ran as fast as her gum-boots and skirts would allow. Her breath was a steamy cloud in front of her face. Her blue eyes were wild.

The German shepherd, a failed airport drug dog who hated crowds and loud noises, and a Blue Heeler, formerly man's best friend, ran along on either side of the frightened woman. They smelled the fear oozing off the woman in waves and kept pace, knowing instinctively that this wasn't the time to chase the myriad of rabbits and deer that scattered before them as they raced through the darkening night. It was in their nature to protect the pack and protect this woman they would, even if it cost them their lives.

Rainbow sprinted towards the one woman she knew could protect her from the madness that had taken over her husband: retired Sergeant Betty Bruce.

The sunset dwindled behind her. She cursed the black curtain of night that descended quickly upon them.

She flew past the moonshine maker's oceanfront home. There were lights on in the shed, but Barney scared her as much as her husband did right now, so she continued on.

Not long afterwards, she saw the moonlight glint off the metal gate that led up to Archie Bruce's house. She knew it well after spending a few days there communicating with Peaches, the poor Jersey cow that had been tasered by a trigger-happy cop, and Peaches buddy, Gertrude, a naughty pot-bellied pig who was always getting into trouble.

She had heard that Betty was living across the road from her father now.

"This way, Blue," she gasped, motioning for the Heeler to join her as she made an abrupt turn to the left, bumping into the shepherd. "Sorry, Bear."

Rainbow jogged up the winding drive. She sighed with relief when she saw that the lights were on in Betty's house on both floors.

Rainbow stomped up the steps to the front porch and then knocked on the door. No one answered. She tried to push the door open in case Betty was upstairs, but it wouldn't budge. The door was locked.

Of course, she reasoned, Betty was used to living in the city and still had big city habits. She still locked the door to their cabin at night, much to her husband's amusement.

She giggled hysterically, realizing she hadn't locked up the cabin when she left this time.

Rainbow circled the house.

She wiped the tears from her eyes and soldiered on.

An ear-piercing squeal and a baritone 'mooooo' met her from the barn. Gertrude raced out to greet her, Peaches following solemnly behind.

"Hey, Gertie, where's your mum," she asked the pot-bellied pig, the two dogs nosing forward cautiously.

Gertrude grunted in answer.

The German shepherd woofed; the Heeler whined.

"Bear, Blue, I'd like you to meet Gertrude and Peaches," Rainbow said, introducing her two dogs to the pot-bellied pig and Jersey cow.

"Gertrude, Peaches, this is Bear and Blue. I expect all of you to behave. No head butting the dogs, Gertie," she ordered the pig as the shepherd sniffed Gertrude's underbelly. It relieved Rainbow that the pig was listening to her.

"And Peaches, no racing off. I won't allow Blue to chase you so ease up on the tension, little girl."

The cow walked forward, her hooves clicking on the cobble stone walkway in front of the barn. Peaches and the Heeler touched noses. The cow bawled and the Heeler jumped backwards.

"Right, you all be good while I knock on the back door."

Rainbow climbed up onto the back porch and peeked through the patio door leading into the kitchen. There were no signs of movement inside. She knocked on the glass, but still there was no answer.

She bit her lip and paced back and forth, unsure of what to do.

Betty could be at her father's house or she could be at the pub. Rainbow didn't have any friends on the island, so Betty and Archie Bruce were the only two choices she had. She liked Archie, but not his buddies. She balked at going to him for help in case one of them was there.

The other reason was that if Frank looked for her, he would immediately try Archie's place and she didn't want to be there if Betty wasn't there and her father was alone. She had seen Frank like this once before when he drank, but even then, the violence in his eyes as he held the axe in one hand and the rope noose in the other was over-the-top.

Rainbow tried opening the back door and patio door of Betty's house, but they were locked too.

Gertrude stood on stubby legs looking up at her. The pig grunted.

"What's that you say, Gert," Rainbow queried the pig.

The pig squealed, grunted and stomped one hoof. She then spun around and waddled back to the barn. Peaches licked her lip and followed her friend.

The dogs sat obediently, wagging their tails and waiting for instructions.

Rainbow wrapped her arms around her waist and shivered. She didn't know what to do but thought Gertrude's offer to share the barn was the safest place for her and the dogs to go.

"Here, boys," she commanded the dogs.

The dogs instantly raced over and sat down beside her.

Rainbow rubbed their ears and under their chins.

"This way," she said, walking purposefully towards the barn. "We're going to take Gertrude up on her offer to stay the night with her."

She entered the small four stall barn and looked around. Hay filled one stall, but the second stall was empty. Dry sawdust and straw covered the floor. The other two stalls were messy, the doors wide open, the pig and cow having free rein to go wherever they wished.

Rainbow laughed. It felt good. She had someplace warm and dry to stay. It eased the tension in her back and shoulders.

Being a pet psychic had its advantages and its disadvantages. Being able to talk with Gertrude tonight made Rainbow feel much better. She knew that the pot-bellied pig and the two dogs would watch over her.

Rainbow entered Gertrude's stall, feeling more secure sleeping in the potbellied pigs stall than the vacant two. The pig nestled down in a gigantic bed of fresh straw. Rainbow snuggled in beside Gertrude, pulled her coat tightly around her slim body, and then patted her lap for the dogs to come in and join her.

Blue jumped at the chance to snuggle and leapt forward, his ears flopping. He plunked himself down in the straw beside Rainbow and then rested his head in her lap.

The German shepherd yawned and circled a few times in the doorway. He laid down, resting his head on his paws, facing outwards, on guard and ready to spring into action if needed.

***

Gertrude nosed the delightfully smelling woman she had invited to stay the night. The delicious scent of yeast, wheat and butter drifted off her coat and skin. That coupled with the pungent scent of sage intermingling with the sweet scents of honey and cinnamon made Gertrude's nose hairs quiver.

It was too bad the woman didn't have a dog biscuit in her pocket given that she had arrived with two foul scented dogs, but the pig was prepared to overlook that given she had helped Gertrude's best friend, Peaches, feel better. Despite the dogs, the woman was welcome to sleep in her bed, whether it was here or across the road.

Gertrude and Peaches had just gotten home from the pub when Gertie heard her friend, Betty, race out of the house and down the driveway.

The pig supposed that she should have gone investigating or should have run after Betty, but she was tired and no one at the pub except for her buddy, Reggie, had paid any attention to her head butts on the window.

What was a pig to do without a pint of draft to help keep her warm on a chilly spring night except to go home to a warm bed of straw?

Gertie sighed and nuzzled the lovely new friend she had made. She may not have had a beer, but this was better than a pint, anyway.

The Bristling Boar

In some part of her mind, the retired Supreme Court judge, Violet Bone, knew she should be afraid, but her fear had turned into anger–righteous anger. Increasingly, as Barney Whyte's trophy wife, Camille, with her perfectly streaked blond hair, manicured nails, and a plethora of overpriced diamond rings on her fingers, continued to prattle on about Vi's refusing to sell her the 'murder' cottage where Vi's sister-in-law was found drowned in her Oscar fish tank, upside down in her knickers. Camille wanted the cottage so she could rent it out for murder weekends. Vi was ready to commit murder right there in the Bristling Boar Pub. The woman just wouldn't stop.

"I don't see why you won't take my money. Like I said before, four hundred thousand is my final offer," Camille stated, her eyes narrowing.

"And like I told you before, Camille," Vi growled, frustrated beyond measure, "my cottage is not for sale, not now, not ever."

"For Pete's sake, leave it alone Cam," Vi's date for the evening, Archie Bruce, whined.

Vi's headache had grown increasingly worse over the evening. The migraine that pummeled her temples had her on edge.

"You know, I like you, Judge Bone. You know how to negotiate. My uncle can negotiate like you. He is one tough cookie," Gwen Mann, the pub owner's wife said amiably.

"Come to think of it, I think he's single, isn't he, honey," the barrel-chested pub owner, Stew Mann, asked his wife.

"Yeah, he is. You two are about the same age too," she agreed, her black bangs bouncing back and forth as she nodded so hard in agreement that she reminded Vi of one of those dogs with the bouncing heads that were all the rage in car decor in the sixties and seventies.

The tiny Malaysian woman was now deep in thought. Vi suspected that she was calculating how much she'd make from such a coupling.

Stew winked at Archie as if Archie were in on some wonderful joke. Vi knew by the stiffening of Archie's shoulders that he wasn't amused either.

"He's a good-looking man and plenty rich," Gwen continued after a moment.

"Yep, Uncle Martin could give you a run for your money, Arch," Stew added, finishing with a chuckle and a wink-wink aimed at his best friend.

"Over my dead body," Archie grimaced.

"He could arrange that too," Gwen chirped.

"But don't worry, we won't ask him too," Stew quickly replied, casting a sideways glance at his wife.

"Thank you, but I celebrate my unmarried old spinsterhood every day," Vi responded casually. In fact, the statement was more than true. Despite several offers and long-term relationships, she had stayed unencumbered.

"Oh, Vi, you're younger than me. You've got plenty of good years left and lots of time to change your mind," Archie blurted out.

"You devil, you do have designs on the Judge, don't you," Barney cried out, pointing a desert fork at his friend.

"Stop it, all of you. You're going to make Vi wish that she had never returned to Seal Island," Archie stuttered. "And she is quite capable of making up her own mind."

"Yeah, you're right, Archie, Judge Bone can make up her own mind and I think my young cousin will do her good," Gwen said forcefully. "I'll call him tomorrow."

Everyone laughed.

The dark cloud that had settled over the little group lifted for a moment.

The door banged open.

Betty suddenly rushed into the pub. She looked around, saw her father and Vi sitting with the Whyte's and the Mann's at a table by the window, and made a beeline for them.

"Angel Puss, what are you doing here," her father asked, rising as his daughter approached the table.

Betty was sweaty and red-faced.

"Is it Peaches? She's not dead, is she," her father hissed, his rheumy eyes watering.

"I knew it. I knew that cop did something to her insides when that jerk tasered her," Stew growled, his fists clenching.

"What? No, Peaches is fine," Betty gasped.

"Then why do you look like someone's died," Barney asked over the rim of his beer glass.

"Oh, I guess I do," Betty stammered, brushing a sweaty strand of hair from her face. "No, I was just… oh, I don't know…"

Vi met Betty's deer in the headlight look head on. She saw Betty bite her lip.

"It's sleeping in that house," Gwen stated bluntly. "It's not good for you. You should sell it and pocket the cash. Buy your own house, one with no ghosts."

"Maybe your wife would like to buy that one," Stew looked pointedly at Barney. "It would be a grand place to run murder mysteries. Think of it… sexy romance writer goes wild and kills all his friends."

Gwen smacked her husband on the arm.

Betty went pale.

Archie glowered.

Camille stuck her nose up in the air.

Vi thought Camille looked like a Pug she used to own.

"Sorry, Betty," Stew blushed, realizing how deeply he had just put his foot in it.

"Pull up a chair, Angel," Archie said to his daughter.

Betty dragged a chair up between Vi and her father. She subconsciously fingered Summer River's diary which she had tucked deep inside one pocket of her over-coat.

"Brenda, bring Betty a beer," Stew called out to one of his staff.

"Thanks, Stew," Betty replied.

A pint of honey pale ale magically appeared in front of Betty within a minute after Stew's call to the pretty young bartender.

Vi noticed the twinkle in Barney's eye as he nodded at the bartender. Unfortunately, his wife did too. Camille picked up a desert fork and looked about to stab her wayward husband with it.

"I don't know what got into me," Betty lied. "I had this awful dream about you, Dad, and woke up thinking it was real."

"And ran all the way here," Barney said, his attention fixed on the bartender. His eyes roved over the bartender's buttocks as she walked away. He reluctantly switched his attention back to Betty.

Barney's sly grin turned into a scowl.

Camille's wrath was threatening to boil over.

Vi saw it all, but now wasn't the time to comment it, no matter how badly she felt like it. Whatever brought Betty down here in a rush was important. She'd discover what it was when there weren't so many people present.

"Ah, that's sweet," Archie said, hugging his daughter.

Betty flushed with embarrassment.

"We were just talking about setting the Judge up with Gwen's cousin or her uncle," Camille said smoothly, "and give your father a run for his money."

"It was all hypothetical, of course," Barney replied, eyeing his wife.

Camille bristled.

"And it went over like quicksand," Vi quipped.

There was a flurry of chuckles around the table.

Betty quietly sipped her beer.

"Anyway, I've had my fill of burgers, beer, and apple pie,' Vi continued. "I must say, Gwen, that your apple pie is the best I have ever had. No wonder your husband has such an ample girth."

Stew patted his stomach as his wife beamed up at him.

"That is a great compliment coming from such an esteemed person as you are, Judge Bone," Gwen replied sincerely.

"And a well deserved one," Archie agreed.

"You must tell me what your secret tip is for making such wonderful fluffy pastry," Vi added.

"Cold hands and…," Gwen confessed.

"A warm heart," her husband added, leaning sideways for a kiss.

"No, silly, it's gingerale," she replied sternly.

The group all laughed and sat back in their chairs.

The silence that ensued was awkward.

"Well, I better be getting Vi home," Archie said, standing up and offering Violet his hand, "and my daughter too by the look of it."

"Thanks, Pops," Betty replied, hastily standing up and almost knocking the table over in the process.

"That must have been some nightmare," Barney quipped.

Betty blushed once again.

"Well, thank you all for the lovely evening," Violet said, feeling anything but happy about the turn of events at the dinner table tonight.

"I think I'll stay and have a night cap," Barney crooned, leaning over to nuzzle his wife's ear.

"Not without me, you won't," Camille said.

"Of course not, sweetheart," Barney agreed.

"Good night all," Vi finished.

Archie, Betty and Vi walked together across the pub. Vi felt as if all eyes in the pub were upon her back. She shivered and looked over her shoulder. Gwen Mann glanced towards her with avarice in her eyes. Camille's eyes glittered with pure hatred.

"You know I think I like my mates better on poker nights," Archie muttered when they reached the parking lot.

"You mean without the wives in tow," Vi asked innocently.

"Something like that," Archie replied, and then scowled.

Archie opened the passenger door of his truck for Betty and Vi to climb in.

Betty scooted into the middle of the bench seat.

Vi accepted Archie's outstretched hand as she climbed up into the old four-by-four pickup truck.

Archie closed the door and went around the truck to the driver's side.

As he did so, Betty leaned towards Vi and whispered in her ear, "I've read some of Summer's diary."

"Oh," Vi whispered back.

Archie opened the driver's door and got in before Betty continued.

"Archie, I know we were going to have a night cap after the pub, but perhaps we can put it off until tomorrow."

"That's okay. I expected that, Vi. If I was married to either of those two women, I might commit Hari-Kari. The pair of them together are evil incarnate, I tell you."

"What did I miss," Betty asked innocently.

"A whole lot of conniving," Betty's father growled.

"I'll fill you in tomorrow, dear," Vi consoled her friend. "Suffice to say that it was an exhausting evening, one that I don't care to repeat."

Archie harrumphed and stared straight ahead as they headed for home.

Tea for Two

Betty's father dropped her off outside the gate in front of his house. She gave him a quick hug before slipping out of the truck and watching him away.

Betty spun on her heel and started walking back down North Shore Road towards Bone's Bailiwick. She knew Vi would be waiting for her.

The clouds had broken up, and it was a beautiful starry night. Pinpricks of light dotted the heavens. The quarter moon cast soft shadows in the woods beside the trail.

The night was frosty.

Betty could see her breath in front of her face.

This time, she didn't have to run and sauntered along, enjoying the feel of the cool crisp air on her face and the tangy taste of salt on her tongue as the breeze pushed the smells and scents of the sea inland.

The cell phone in her pocket rang. She pulled it out and saw Tom Powder's name illuminated on the screen.

"Hi, Tom," she said briskly into the phone.

"Bet, what's up," his baritone voice echoed through the stillness of the night.

Betty turned down the cell's volume.

"The new owner of Summer River's farm found Summer's old diary under the bed and she gave it to me. I've only read part of it, but I discovered why Summer filed a paternity suit against Andy."

"And?" Powder asked.

"And she was terrified of the baby's father. She asked Andy if he could help her. He suggested that she file a very public paternity suit against him to protect herself once it became obvious that she

13

was pregnant."

"And did she reveal who the father was," Powder queried.

"Wait... wait... wait for it," Betty joked with the good-natured inspector.

"She didn't, did she?"

Betty chuckled.

"Not yet, but I haven't finished the whole diary. She was reluctant to file the paternity suit, but Andy insisted upon it. Andy said that he would make a big hullaballoo over the lawsuit and that they would settle out of court for a million dollars just before the case went to trial so it would be recorded in the court records if anyone looked. It seemed neither of them cared about the money, only that it looked legit and would take the heat off Summer."

"So, there was no mention of where the million dollars went?"

"Not from what I read. I never went over any of her banking records, but maybe you could?"

Betty sighed wistfully. She wished that Summer or Andy had come to her about this whole mess. Betty knew she could have protected Summer from whoever it was that Summer was afraid of.

"Why don't I pop over to the island in a few days and I can take your statement and record the diary into evidence? I'll need it to subpoena any financial records."

"Give me a little more time than that, Tom," Betty pleaded. "I know I've just retired, plus I was removed from this case, but I deserve that much."

"Only if you'll have dinner with me when I get there," Inspector Powder teased her.

Betty laughed merrily, her eyes twinkling at the thought of the handsome, almost divorced, Native inspector with a smile to die for and coal black hair that she wouldn't mind running her fingers through.

"Done," she agreed.

"All right call me when you're ready but be careful. Summer River is dead, and she was frightened of someone who obviously lived on that island," Powder cautioned her.

"I will," she promised him, ending the call.

Betty let her breath out slowly. She wondered if she could keep that promise.

***

Betty knocked on the door of Violet Bone's cottage.

"Good timing, the kettle has boiled, and the tea is steeping," the older woman said to the newly retired RCMP Sergeant standing at her door.

"Hmmm," Betty said as she walked in. "That smells like some of Summer's Mint Melody."

"It is," Vi agreed. "I will miss those teas once they're all done. I hoped that the new owners of her farm might continue making them."

"I think a lot of people were," Betty concurred, slipping her boots and coat off. She tucked the boots up against the wall and hung her jacket up on a peg, slipping Summer's diary out of a pocket as she did so.

"So, the plot thickens," Violet murmured as she poured two cupfuls of aromatic mint tea.

"Let's go sit by the fire in the living room," Vi continued. "It's still a tad drafty in the rest of the house."

Betty accepted a cup of tea from the semi-retired Supreme Court Judge and the two of them made their way into the living room from the open style country kitchen.

Betty's cheeks glowed from the dry warmth that the fire crackling in the iron woodstove exuded. She noticed that her father had stacked a good day's worth of wood on the iron rack beside the stove so that Vi didn't have to go outside in the dark to retrieve any. She smiled. Her father was a kind man.

Betty sat down in one of the comfortable, over-stuffed leather armchairs. She propped her feet up on a stool and tucked the diary down beside one leg and sipped her tea.

Vi collapsed in an old Lazy boy chair and tucked a quilt over her lap before taking a long sip of her tea.

The two ladies sat in companionable silence for a while, drinking tea, and watching the logs burn inside the woodstove.

Betty took a deep breath, pulled out the diary, and opened to a page she had tagged with a piece of tissue.

"Are you ready for this," Betty asked her friend and investigative partner.

"As ready as I'll ever be," Vi whispered.

***

June 15

I am so afraid.

I haven't felt fear like this since my parents died and Moon's anger sank to even darker depths and depravities.

That was almost twelve years ago.

Was I really so young and naïve as to think I could have it all?

Am I too proud?

As I sit in my garden with Sir Percival purring in my lap, I cannot help but wonder at this.

I love the earth, working in it, my fingers sifting through it. I love growing my plants, watching the buds burst forth, the smell of the flowers and the buzz of the bees. There is nothing better than working in the barn, mixing the teas, the scents of jasmine, mint, honeysuckle and rosehips making my senses sing.

With his help, I became so successful.

As I look up at the blue sky and the upraised arms of the stone angel upon wish I lean, I can only wish that my child yet unborn get a chance to feel this beauty, this passion for all things living, and yet I feel too like my life is but a kite in a hurricane, bucking and straining until the string that holds it breaks and it disappears into the raging sky.

It's not entirely his fault, though. I am as much to blame...I think.

I'm not sure anymore.

Life is full of hard lessons. Don't drink and drive. Don't plant before April 1st. Don't plan on a wet summer. Don't plan on a dry summer. Don't rely on anyone but yourself.

And...don't fall in love. Never, ever fall in love. It hurts too much when it's gone.

I'm not sure I'll ever trust anyone ever again. Well, maybe Andy. The court case finished today, and he put a million clams into my bank account.

Not sure what I'll do with all those greenbacks?

Maybe I'll mulch it into the garden. Oh, wait… the ink is toxic. Okay, maybe I'll just burn it.

I'd ask him what to do about it, but I don't trust him anymore and I'm afraid… so damn afraid.

I have to think of the baby.

I have to think positive thoughts, lest my daughter or my son come out like my brother.

Positive thoughts… like the bees pollinating the flowers, the sun on my face, and the feel of Sir Percival's soft fur beneath my fingers. Yes, that's it.

I'll burn that cool million.

It will be cathartic. I'll flip the bird at the God of Avarice.

I feel better already.

Oh, Jeez, this morning sickness sucks. I got to go puke now.

***

"A couple of days before this, Summer wrote that she thought Andy's solution to her abject fear of the baby's father was to file a paternity suit against Andy and then settle out of court right before it became obvious that she was pregnant," Betty advised Vi, and then took a sip of tea.

"And she obviously never revealed who the father was yet," Vi responded, her brow furrowing as she contemplated the words the dead girl had written in her diary not too long before her untimely death.

"No, she didn't. She just refers to the father as 'him'."

"Interesting what she had to say about her brother, Moon," Vi mused aloud.

"Makes you wonder what type of depravities she was talking about. I know he was always an angry kid. Everyone blamed it on the guff he took at school for his name."

"Yes, naming a child, Moon River, especially a boy, was thoughtless," Vi agreed.

"It was nice to discover the reason behind Summer's filing of the paternity suit against Andy though," Betty remarked. She let out a lengthy sigh of relief. "I just wish they'd come to me about it."

"I'm sure Andy would have, but he didn't want to break Summer's confidence in him, plus you were dating. He may not have been sure how you'd take it," Vi consoled her friend.

"That's true, I guess."

"Tell me. Do you know who helped Summer build up her business? I had thought she did it all on her own," Vi said, looking at Betty over the brim of her teacup.

"I know that Barney helped her out financially and introduced her teas to a few spa owners he knew, but my dad helped her put up all the deer fencing and I think Reggie taught her what he knew about... how shall I say it?"

"Farming," Vi responded.

"Farming," Betty agreed.

The two ladies laughed, their eyes twinkling at the thought of the old fisherman slowly explaining how he grew his prize cannabis to the inexperienced hippie girl.

"Andy was a friend of Summer's fiancé, I believe," Betty continued, her smile fading. "It was devastating for her when he died so close to her losing her parents."

"Hence her words: *Don't fall in love. Never, ever fall in love. It hurts too much when it's gone.*"

"I expect so," Betty mumbled, knowing all too well how much it hurt to lose someone you loved. She couldn't imagine how Summer had coped.

Betty and Summer weren't that different, except in age. Betty was a lot older than Summer when she finally found love again after a disastrous and abusive marriage. Andy had renewed her faith in trust and released a passion inside of her she didn't know existed. It broke her heart when he died, even more so to think of him as a killer. She wished that Summer had lived long enough to realize that broken hearts healed and to experience the joy of being a mother.

"You know I think we're going to have to continue this tomorrow, Betty," Vi drawled, her eyelids fluttering closed. "I'm exhausted. Between those two money grabbing women at the pub and this mystery, I feel drained."

"I'm not surprised," Betty announced, shutting the diary with a dull 'thwap'. "We'll discuss it tomorrow and read more of this diary."

Vi went to stand up, but Betty motioned her to stay where she was.

"Do bring Gertie and Peaches when you come, I've missed them," Vi waved to her friend.

"Will do."

Percival strolled into the room, tail in the air. His yellow cat's eyes regarded Betty with suspicion. She regarded him back, equally suspicious that the big bundle of fluff would attack her. He was a funny cat and only took to certain people. He bonded to Vi, the minute he met her, and he seemed to like her father just as much, but Betty, the cat had decided was a mortal enemy.

"Look after your mum, Percy," Betty said to the cat.

"Oh, he will. He's a wonderful boy," Vi crooned to the former barn cat.

The cat flicked his tail in response and then sauntered across the room. He stopped to lick himself and then leapt onto Vi's lap.

"Just one thing before I go, Vi," Betty said. She bit her lip, wondering if she should tell the judge who she believed the father to be.

"What's that," Vi murmured.

The old judge absently stroked the fluffy Persian, her eyes closing.

"Nothing," Betty shrugged. "I just wanted to say that I'm glad you're back and if you need anything, just call."

The judge smiled as she drifted off to sleep

Betty grinned and made her way to the door.

She thought more about what she had just read: *The court case finished today, and he put a million clams into my bank account. Not sure what I'll do with all those greenbacks?*

Did Summer really pull a million dollars out of the bank? If so, what did she do with it? Was it in a suitcase under her bed? Was it buried somewhere on the farm? Or did she burn it like she said she would do?

A million dollars in cold hard cash was definitely enough money to kill for.

The Sleep-Over

The German shepherd watched over the sleeping form of the very nice human who had saved it from a life of loneliness, scents so fowl that sometimes they burned its nostrils, and noise so loud that it made it pee for no reason.

He hated that noise, the noise of too many people in one place, the thrumming of conveyer belts, and the roar of giant jets. He also hated how a lot of humans looked at him, except for his two handlers, of course. His handlers were nice and always brought him treats. One of his handlers used to laugh and laugh when she scratched his belly and he thumped his tail with glee.

The humans in the crowds at the airport would dart away from him, the sour smell of sweat oozing off them in stinking waves. Many looked at him with fear and loathing, when he all he was doing was being a good dog and doing his job. It wasn't all bad though. He loved it when the human puppies raced up to him and threw their arms around him. They smelled yummy, and they oozed love. For some reason, the humans with them always got mad when he licked the human puppy's faces.

Living with the nice human who now slept with the interesting smelling creature with the funny face and his other dog friend was much better. He had yearned for one human, just like this one, who he could protect and follow like an obedient dog should.

Life on the farm with the human female and her mate was wonderful. There were rabbits and rats to chase, interesting things to sniff, and the only noise was the twitter of birds and the wind in the trees.

Lately, though, his hackles were up. There was danger at the farm. He sensed rather than saw it.

There was something wrong with the man at the farm. He smelled *sweet and sour at the same time. There was something else in the smell too, and it was nasty. He smelled like one of things that a good dog should tell his handler about by lying down. He kept lying down and trying to let the human woman know that he smelled the 'bad' thing on her mate, but she didn't understand him. The man got loud when he smelled like that and he waved his hands in the air and sometimes Bear saw him in the barn talking to invisible humans.*

Bear was glad that the human female had run into the night with him to protect her after the angry man burst through the door. He knew his friend would try to protect her too, but he wasn't trained in combat like Bear was.

The shepherd relaxed. He listened to the soft snores coming from the stall in which the sleeping forms lay.

The human woman was curled up, one arm flung over the interesting creature's neck, her head resting on top of its head. His friend stretched out beside the human, his head resting in her lap. They slept peacefully.

The shepherd closed his eyes, content.

Footsteps crunched on the gravel outside the barn.

The dog's ears perked up, and he listened as the footsteps grew louder.

He growled low in his chest, careful not to alarm his sleeping charges, but alerting the intruder he was there and ready to defend his friends.

He stood up, nostrils quivering, every nerve in his body stretched taut.

A narrow beam of light roved over the entrance to the barn, coming closer and closer still. It got brighter as the intruder approached.

He prepared himself for battle and crouched down low, his lips pealed back to reveal his incisors.

A human woman rounded the corner.

The glare from the flashlight blinded him.

He was about to launch himself at the intruder when she said without the scent of fear or malice: "And who might you be?"

He stopped growling and sat down.

This woman reminded him of his handlers. An air of authority sur-

rounded her. It was in her voice and in her stance. This was a human used to being obeyed by good dogs like him.

He wagged his tail.

***

Betty looked down at the beautiful black and tan German shepherd standing in her barn, his hackles raised, his haunches and shoulders bunched, a low growl emanating from deep within his chest.

A deep set of intelligent eyes regarded her. While the shepherd was in protection mode, she knew that the dog was looking for assurance that she wasn't a threat.

Betty smiled.

"And who might you be," she queried the dog.

She saw the shepherd visibly relax.

She wondered whose dog it was. By the glossiness of his coat and the keen look in his eye, he was not a stray. Strays were unusual on the island, but not unheard of. Some people used Seal Island as a dumping ground for unwanted dogs, but mostly in the summer when the marina was busy. Sometimes dogs would jump ship in the harbor and get lost in the hills, leaving their families bereft and heartbroken. These dogs were simple to return home, as most had microchips. Perhaps this was one such dog?

"So beautiful, what are you doing in my barn? Are you a recent friend of Gert and Peaches," she asked gently, not wanting to worry the dog.

Peaches heard her name and poked her nose out of her stall door. She nuzzled the dog and then looked bleary-eyed at Betty, the flashlight's beam bouncing off her liquid brown eyes. Satisfied that nothing was amiss, the cow returned to her stall and stuffed her face in a manger full of hay.

The dog looked from the cow to Betty and then Gertrude's stall to Betty.

"Ah, Gertrude's having a sleep-over," Betty chortled, amused, catching the dog's drift.

Betty lowered her hand for the dog to sniff her. The dog whimpered and wagged his tail as it did so.

"Good dog. Good boy," she crooned.

The dog rolled over and exposed its tummy.

"Aren't you a sweetheart?"

Betty laughed lightly and rubbed the shepherd's stomach.

"Right, let's see who's visiting our barn," she whispered to the dog.

The German shepherd wagged its tail and followed her into Gertrude's stall.

Betty smothered a laugh when she saw the colorfully dressed pet psychic curled up with the pot-bellied pig and another grey and black dog peppered with white splotches, all three sleeping peacefully.

The German shepherd brushed past her and stood casually by her side, looking down at the strange scene.

The dog yawned.

"It's been a long night for you, has it? Yeah, me too."

Betty patted the dog's head and then crept away.

"Stay," she ordered the shepherd. "I'll be back."

Betty left the barn.

She idly wondered who instigated the sleep-over in the barn, her pig or the pet psychic. Either way, despite the warmth that the pig threw off, it was too cold to be sleeping out in the open like that.

Betty retrieved two old blankets from the house and returned to the barn.

The German shepherd greeted her like they were long lost friends. She grinned. The dog reminded her of some RCMP canine dogs she had met. He had that same calm intelligence about him. She had a deep respect for those dogs and the officers in the Canine Unit.

"Come on, let's keep your master warm," she said.

Betty walked into Gertrude's stall and draped a large woolen blanket over the sleeping woman and the other dog. The Heeler looked up and wagged its tail.

Betty could have sworn that the dog winked at her.

She chuckled and then folded up the other blanket. She placed it on the cement floor just outside the stall door.

"Here you go, big guy," she said to the shepherd, bending down and patting the blanket.

The dog wagged its tail and licked her under the chin. Betty grinned and patted the blanket once again. The dog finally lay down and curled into a ball on the soft blanket.

"See you in the morning, champ," she finished, standing up.

Betty drew the barn door shut behind her. The woman was sleeping in Gertrude's stall for a reason. She could have woken her up and asked her into the house, but between the two dogs and Gertrude, the pet psychic was well protected. Whoever had frightened her enough to put her there would be hard pressed to get past the animals.

***

Rainbow awoke to the sound of scratching.

She opened her eyes; the pot-bellied pig and cow were nowhere to be seen. Blue scratched behind his ear with his right hind paw for all he was worth. The German shepherd seemed to have abandoned her as well.

She looked at the crumpled blue woolen blanket that covered her and yawned. There was a note tacked to the wall of the stall.

"Coffee's on," was all it said.

She kissed her Heeler on the nose and stood up, straightening out her coat and picking out some errant shavings that had become embedded in the woolen weave.

She did a few quick stretches at the waist to work out the kinks and then signaled for Blue to join her as she ambled towards the house.

The serene beauty of the sun rising on the fields and her dog scampering around the yard made her wonder if last night was real. She could see Gertrude and Peaches grazing amongst a herd of deer in the distance.

Obviously, Betty had found her asleep amongst the animals in the barn and covered her with the blanket. She was stiff, but the wool blanket and the animals had kept her warm.

The nightmare scene in the farmhouse kitchen set her mind to reeling.

Did Frank really burst into the house with an axe in hand yelling that the real money was in murder and not in chickens?

Rainbow trudged up the two stairs to the back patio, her heart heavy.

She looked through the patio door into Betty's kitchen and saw the German shepherd sleeping on a blanket by the door, looking every bit the gentleman. She hadn't ever seen the shepherd look that peaceful.

"Here, Blue," she called, patting her leg.

The Blue Heeler cavorted towards her, ears flapping, tongue lolling to one side. The dog's eyes were bright. A brilliant yellow aura surrounded the happy animal.

Rainbow knocked and then slid the door open.

Bear stretched and stood up to greet her, his tail windmilling around and around.

Betty stood at the stove, spatula in hand. Steam rose from the scrambled eggs and homemade hash browns in the skillets as she gently flipped them over. Her silver and blond hair cascaded freely around her face, her blue eyes sparkling with mirth as she looked over her shoulder at the disheveled, red faced, dread locked hippy standing in her doorway.

"Come in," she greeted Rainbow warmly. "Coffee's hot and the eggs and hash browns are nearly done. Perfect timing. I was going to send Champ out to get you."

Rainbow was about to tell her she didn't drink coffee, but her mouth watered at the delicious scent of cinnamon and vanilla that drifted through the kitchen.

"Thank you," Rainbow replied, bravely. "I see that Bear has made himself at home."

"Is that his name," Betty inquired. "I've been calling him Champ."

The shepherd wagged his tail and licked Rainbow's hand. She gave him a quick kiss on the nose and then made her way to the coffee pot.

Blue whined at the patio door.

"Let your other dog in. The more the merrier," Betty said good-naturedly.

"Oh, thank you so much," Rainbow gushed.

Rainbow hated hearing the timid squeak in her voice. It wasn't always like that.

Her host was doing everything possible to make her feel at ease. Not everyone would be so nice to someone they found sleeping with their pig in the barn.

Rainbow opened the door, and the Heeler plowed through it. The German shepherd woofed loudly, and the other dog sat down obediently.

"Next thing you know, Gertrude will be rushing in. Good thing I'm not cooking bacon," the retired policewoman joked, taking down four plates from the cupboard.

Rainbow smiled as she returned to the coffee pot and poured herself of a mug of steaming hot coffee.

"There's honey on the counter and cream in the fridge if you want any."

"Black is fine," Rainbow whispered.

Betty held up the large skillet of scrambled eggs. She tipped it sideways and divided it into four portions on the plates. She then split the hash browns up into five portions, leaving the fifth pile of potatoes in the skillet.

"I'm sorry, I didn't know you were expecting company," Rainbow stuttered, stricken by the thought of strangers coming in and seeing her in such a state.

"Oh, no, these two plates are for the dogs," Betty replied gleefully. "The rest of the potatoes are for Gertie. She loves hash browns in the morning."

Rainbow giggled. The giggle turned into a hearty laugh. A dam of pent-up emotions gave way.

Betty placed the two plates of eggs and potatoes on the table and looked at the baleful dogs looking expectantly at her.

"Wait until your breakfast is cool," she said to the dogs, pointing a warning finger at them. The dogs lied down quietly on the floor and watched her every move.

"I don't know what to say, except thank-you yet again," Rainbow gushed.

"No problem. I've enjoyed Champ's company. You must tell me all about him and what brought you here, but not until after we eat. I had a rough night myself, although, I expect not as rough as yours."

It was then that Rainbow noticed the sunken look around Betty's eyes and the stress lines around her mouth. She felt awful for adding more stress to this woman's life.

"Eat up or the dogs will have a really big breakfast," Betty ordered her guest before slathering everything on her plate with ketchup.

***

Betty sat with the pet psychic on the back-porch drinking coffee while the German shepherd, Blue Heeler, and pot-bellied pig dug into their breakfasts. The race was on. It was a toss-up as to who finished first.

The animals played musical plates until they were satisfied that not a speck of egg or potato was left uneaten. Tummies full, the two dogs and the pig raced back into the pasture to start a game of chase the cow. The cow didn't seem to mind and cavorted with the two dogs like they had been friends since birth.

"So, begin at the beginning and tell me what happened,' Betty advised Rainbow.

Rainbow took a deep breath and let it out.

Slowly, she began to tell her story.

***

Blue whined at the door until I let him in.

Blue is my husband's dog, not mine. Frank's had Blue since he was eight weeks old. He and Bear were out in the back pasture with Frank when you came over to pick up the diary.

"What's wrong, Blue," I asked the agitated dog as he bolted through the doorway.

Bear had been sleeping peacefully by the woodstove in the living room and he came racing in to see what was happening. Blue ran up to the shepherd, instinctively rolling onto his back in submission. Bear whined and nosed the other dog.

Blue got up and started pacing the room, but after a few laps dove under the kitchen table and wouldn't come out.

"It's okay, buddy. When you want to talk about it, I'm here for you," I said to the shaking dog, but he didn't answer.

I shrugged and went back to work kneading the ball of dough that I was working on. Bear went back to lie down by the warmth of the fire.

Suddenly, the kitchen door crashed open.

I gasped and spun around.

I must have really let loose with a cry of despair in my mind because Bear came flying into the kitchen barking and growling.

I silenced the dog with a hand signal by lowering my hand, palm flat, indicating that he should lie down. Bear responded instantly, like he was trained to do. Blue continued to whimper under the table.

I didn't even recognize the man standing the doorway. My husband was a total stranger. He just stood there, an axe in one hand, a hang-man's noose in the other, bootless. His aura was an angry shade of red with black bullet holes in it.

This couldn't be my Frank, but it was.

Blue found his courage and wiggled out from under the table. He stood beside Bear and growled at the man he loved more than anything else in the world.

I was terrified and knew I was in trouble.

I didn't know if Frank would swing the axe at the dogs...or me.

"I've got it, honey, I know exactly how we're going to make this farm work," Frank spat at me. "Forget the birds. Murder is where the money is. I've got it all worked out."

Then Frank spun on his heel, his muddy socks slipping on the wood floor, and he headed back to the barn.

I didn't even realize until that moment that I was still holding the bread dough in one hand.

Anyway, I threw it on the counter, quickly wiped my hands, grabbed my jacket and headed for the door.

I called the dogs, and we ran for it. You were the only person who I could think of who would know what to do.

***

"And here you are," Betty mumbled.

"And here I am," Rainbow repeated.

Betty stared at Watchtower Mountain in the distance. The sun glistened off its snowy peak.

The dogs tired of their game of chase the cow and left Peaches in peace and returned to the house. Gertrude returned and disappeared into the barn.

"Does your husband have a history of mental illness or drug abuse," she asked the distraught woman.

"No, never," Rainbow gasped.

Betty sensed that there was something more that the pet psychic wasn't telling her.

"You said that Champ, er, Bear, was a drug dog. Are you sure he wasn't reacting to something that he smelled on Frank?"

"Frank wasn't Frank anymore, not in that moment. Bear was being naturally protective, but when Blue was ready to defend me too, that was all the confirmation that I needed."

Betty sat back in her chair, thinking about Andy and his uncharacteristic rage when he tried to kill Vi and her father. This sounded so similar that it was eerie.

The shepherd nosed her hand. She absently stroked his head.

The Heeler settled under the table, resting its head on Rainbow's feet.

"Frank had trouble with alcohol a long time ago. He had been clean and sober for four years before we met. He knows how I feel about booze," Rainbow admitted. "I was mad when your father and two of his buddies showed up at my door unasked for carrying bottles of wine, a case of beer, and some mason jars filled with moonshine."

"What," Betty gasped. "When?"

"It was several weeks ago. Your father was nice about it and apologized when I told him we didn't drink. He asked me if I could help Peaches. I was delighted. That's how I ended up getting to know Gertrude," Rainbow admitted innocently, "and you too, of course."

Betty felt the hair rise on the back of her neck. The only two men that she could think of who would have showed up unannounced with her father was Stew Mann and Barney Whyte.

It was all starting to add up.

First, the love of her life, Andy McDowell, admitted to murdering three women in the most bizarre of ways while in a homicidal rage, only to be thwarted by a protective pot-bellied pig named Gertrude.

Second, the coroner discovered that Andy was suffering from severe lead poisoning and was high on a potent and deadly form of LSD. No drugs were ever found, nor was anything that could have caused the lead poisoning ever found either.

Third, Rainbow discovered Summer's diary after buying Summer's farm. Summer died in the arms of a stone angel, the result of a fall from the barn roof trying to fix a faulty lightning rod on a sunny day. In that diary Summer revealed her fear of the baby's father and that Andy offered to help by creating a fake paternity suit in order to protect Summer. That meant that the father of Summer's unborn baby lived on the island.

Fourth, there may be a million dollars in cash stored somewhere on Summer's, and now Rainbow and Frank's, property and a million bucks is more than enough money to kill for.

Fifth, Stew Mann admitted to being in love with Tiffany Hyde-White, a bestselling sex addicted recovering alcoholic murder/mystery writer who died in the garden with her gnomes after eating peanut laced chocolates. Stew told Vi that he would have left his wife for her if Tiffany felt the same, but she was in love with Betty's ex-husband. Tiffany had warned Betty about Andy and wanted to reveal a secret, but never had the chance. She was also deathly allergic to peanuts and everyone on the island knew it.

Sixth, Gwen Mann was a jealous woman with a history of violence, one who wouldn't let any woman get between her and her man.

Seventh, Barney and Camille Whyte loved money and their extravagant lifestyle. Camille ignored Barney's many affairs so long as they didn't interfere with her shopping sprees.

Eighth, Barney made moonshine.

Ninth, Barney bought the stone angel for Summer.

Tenth, Barney, Reggie Phoenix, and her father, helped Summer get her business going. Summer wrote in her diary she was terrified of 'him', the man who helped her get started and who also appeared to be the father of her unborn baby.

Betty blanched. She glanced over at the pet psychic. She had the uneasy feeling that what was going on at the McDonald Farm might be the key to solving the mysterious deaths of two of her friends, her lover, and Summer River.

The German shepherd looked her in the eye. It was almost as if the dog knew what she was thinking.

"Let's go have a chat with your husband, shall we," Betty said, pushing away from the table.

The shepherd stood up. Betty saw him look to her for guidance. It was the same intense stare that she had seen police dogs give their human partners.

"I think he's bonded to you," Rainbow said, watching the dog's movements. The dog never took his eyes off of Betty. "He has to go back to work at the airport again soon and I am afraid for him. He hates it. I've been trying to find a suitable person to adopt him, but every time I think I found someone the airport authorities won't approve them. If he continues to not work out, I'm afraid they might put him down."

Betty smirked. She didn't need another pet, but she also knew that drug dogs and police dogs retired from service had to go to specialized homes if one of their handlers or the police officer who worked with them didn't take them. Even when retired, these dogs needed a job to be happy. Now that she was working as a special consultant with the force, a trained drug sniffing German shepherd might be a handy partner to have around.

"Give me the name of your contact and I'll think about it. In the meantime, Bear has a job to do," Betty added, rubbing the dog under the chin.

"And what is that?" Rainbow asked with a shiver.

"Protecting you."

Hog Gone Wild

The two women were quite an odd sight even for Seal Island as they walked up North Shore Road accompanied by a thousand-pound Jersey cow, a two hundred pound pot-bellied pig, an eighty pound German shepherd, and a fifty pound Blue Heeler.

The Heeler constantly tried to herd the cow, but the pig would have none of it and ran the dog off every time it tried.

The shepherd walked at a heel beside Betty even though the dog was off leash and welcome to join in the fun the pig, the cow, and the Heeler, seemed to be having.

Betty wore her hair tied back beneath a blue ball cap with an embroidered mounted member of the RCMP Musical Ride on the bill, beige slacks tucked into her worn brown RCMP issue knee high riding boots, regulation issue, and a red and black lumberjack shirt. The German shepherd striding by her side only added to the mystic she chose to create.

Neither she nor Rainbow knew what they would find when they reached Rainbow's farm, but Betty felt a casual visit and a reminder that the law wasn't that far away might be in order.

Slate grey clouds hung low in the sky, but so far the rain that threatened had held off. A breeze blew down the Strait of Georgia, rustling the budding leaves in the poplar and maple trees that lined the road. The scent of conifers hung in the air. It was a typical spring day on the coast.

Betty noticed Barney Whyte standing in his garden taking a leak in one of the bushes.

"Afternoon, Barney," Betty drawled.

"Top of the day to you, ladies," the billionaire moonshine maker replied, unabashed at being caught in such a precarious situation.

The German shepherd sniffed the air. A baritone growl rumbled from deep inside its chest, and then the dog did something odd. The shepherd walked over to the fence, close to where Barney continued to water the bushes, and lied down in the gravel at the side of the road.

Betty stopped dead in her tracks.

"Bear, no, come back here," Rainbow stuttered, blushing from head to foot.

The shepherd ignored her. Instead, the dog stood up, looked Betty in the eye and then lay down again.

"Bear...," Rainbow patted her leg, exasperated that the dog wouldn't listen to her.

"Its okay, Rainbow," Betty said to the worried young woman.

Rainbow gave her a questioning look. Betty put a finger to her lips. Rainbow nodded in understanding.

Betty was a bit surprised by the dog's action, but not completely so. She had suspected Barney of imbibing in more than just beer and moonshine for some time now. The shepherd may have had difficulties with his job at the airport, but the dog was doing it now.

Had Barney Whyte graduated to hard drugs? Had he maybe developed a taste for LSD? If so, would he give up his supplier so Betty could see if the drugs were a match to what was in Andy's system?

Betty already suspected that Barney was the father of Summer's child. If so, what was he capable of? Murder, perhaps? Or was the dog's reaction to the man taking a piss in the bushes just over-protectiveness?

"Good dog," Betty told the shepherd. She pulled three Milk Bones from her pocket. She gave one to the shepherd and one each to the pig and the other dog.

"Bear doesn't like him," Rainbow whispered into Betty's ear.

"That's because Bear's a good judge of character," Betty whispered back.

"Nice to see you out and about, Rainbow," Barney chirped, zipping up his fly. "I see you've picked up a few more critters. Watch out for that pig, she's a killer, you know."

Rainbow gasped.

"That's enough, Barney," Betty growled.

Rainbow eyed the pig dubiously.

"Oooh, the young lady doesn't know, does she," the silver haired man quipped. "Well, stop by for a shot of hooch some time and I'll tell you a tale about a hog gone wild. The story's got a cliff hanger ending. Oh, I forgot, you don't imbibe. Well I'm sure we can find something of interest."

Betty glowered. She hadn't expected such a slap in the face this early in the day, especially from a friend of her father's. What had changed in the last few days? Was it the dinner at the pub last night? Did Betty's suspicions show on her face? Had she given herself away some how?

Betty decided there was no time like the present to shake things up a little bit.

"Interesting thing just happened on our walk this morning," Betty said, keeping her voice chipper and up-beat.

"Oh," Barney replied, resting his arms on the fence and leaning over it, his ruddy face flushing as he broke into a wide grin.

Gertrude raced over to say 'hello', but Barney unceremoniously brushed her snout away.

The German shepherd growled.

The Blue Heeler barked.

Peaches stopped to chew some early rose buds off a wild rose bush.

An exasperated Rainbow grabbed the Heeler by the collar and wagged a finger in its face. The dog instantly stopped barking. She then turned to the shepherd, but Betty gently tugged Rainbow away from the shepherd.

Rainbow looked at Betty in confusion.

"Bear, heel," Betty commanded the dog. The shepherd ran to her and sat by her side, a small whine escaping its lips.

"Yes, the interesting thing is that this shepherd is a trained drug sniffing dog and he doesn't seem to like you, Barney. In fact, he just indicated to me that he smells drugs on you now."

"Is that a fact," was the older man's guarded response.

"It is," Betty smirked.

"Then it's a good thing that you don't have a badge anymore, isn't it," Barney remarked, his voice taking on a sharp edge.

Betty blushed.

"Still, it's probable cause," she jibed, her words razor sharp.

"Hmmmm, but it will take hours to get a warrant and even more hours to get here and by that time my lawyers will block the warrant and you won't find anything anyway," he drawled.

The two of them faced off.

Barney chuckled and winked at her.

"Good day to you, Barney," Betty drawled. She had the answer she needed. Barney wasn't just dealing in moonshine, but hard drugs as well, possibly even LSD. As for her other questions, time would tell.

"And a good day to you, former Sgt. Beatrice Bruce," the old man added, turning away and gambling across the yard to his backyard brewery.

Betty inhaled sharply and then let out her breath slowly to ease the pressure in her chest. Barney Whyte thought he was above the law, but no one was, not in this country anyway.

"Can you explain to me what just happened and why that nasty man called Gertrude a killer," Rainbow asked gently.

"Because she is," Betty responded.

"Am I safe with her," the young woman stammered, distancing herself from both Gertrude and Betty. "Am I safe with you?"

"That's a good question right now. If you have any doubts about staying at home when we get there, I'm going to take you to Judge Bone's house. You'll be more than welcome there and Vi has developed an affinity for Summer River's teas. You'll have lots to talk about. She was hoping that you'd start up the tea farm again. Her cat may voice some objections over the dogs being there, but Percival's a tough old barn cat and he'll get used to them."

"You're evading my other question though. Am I safe around Gertrude?"

"No, I'm not evading anything," Betty said soothingly. "Gertrude saved my life and my father's and Judge Bone's too. Unfortunately to do that she head butted the man I loved over a cliff. He confessed to murdering my friend, Eliza, Judge Bone's sister-in-law, and my friend, Tiffany, as well as the former owner of your farm."

"Summer was murdered," she gasped in horror.

"The coroner ruled Summer's death accidental, the same as he ruled the other two deaths, but I've never been convinced of that."

"Maybe that's why she's still there," Rainbow gulped.

"Who's still there," Betty queried as they started walking up the road once more, their menagerie following enthusiastically behind them.

"Please don't think I'm crazy, but Summer's ghost is the one who showed me where her diary was and she's been visiting the farm and…, well, and you too," Rainbow confessed, brushing her dreadlocks back under the scarf she had tied around her head.

"I don't think you're crazy at all," Betty answered. "Well, not completely."

Betty grinned.

Rainbow chuckled.

"Okay, I suppose I might appear to be a little strange to some people," Rainbow agreed.

Betty roared with laughter. Rainbow joined in. The dogs barked and wagged their tails, eager to join in the joke. Not to be outdone, Gertrude head-butted the Heeler good-naturedly.

The women's gale of laughter turned into amused chuckles as they continued on their journey.

Betty listened to the birds trilling in the trees. A couple of bald eagles circled in the sky overhead.

"That man," Rainbow asked, somewhat reticent, "he has a really smoky aura and he frightens me. He was in a lot of pictures on the wall at our house when we first got there. I packed them all away. They're in boxes in the barn. Should I be afraid of him?"

"Yes,' Betty replied simply.

"What about your father and that other man, the one who owns the pub," she continued.

"My father is harmless and you can trust him. Stew is a letch, but I think he's harmless too. If you can't get hold of me or my dad, then find either Vi Bone or Reggie Phoenix. Reggie owns *The Persephone*. She's docked down at the harbour. He has property on South Shore Road too, but the boat is the best bet."

"Reggie Phoenix? Is he that friendly fellow with the grey beard and piercing blue eyes that looks like he should be in an Old Spice cologne commercial?"

"Yep, that's Reggie," Betty chortled.

"He's hilarious. He has the most brilliant white aura that I've ever seen," Rainbow gushed.

Betty burst out laughing again.

At that moment a herd of wild sheep charged across the road in front of them.

Peaches bawled a warning.

Gertrude charged a ram.

The dogs went nuts.

Betty and Rainbow chased after the dogs in two different directions.

Old McDonald Had a Farm

Rainbow and Betty approached the metal gate that was fastened by a slip chain at the end of the drive leading up to Rainbow's farm.

"I think we'll leave Gert and Peaches outside the gate. I don't want them trampling your garden and Peaches eats everything in sight," Betty remarked.

"Probably a good idea," Rainbow agreed, pushing open the gate while Betty shooed the pig and cow away.

Gertrude was none too pleased when she saw that the German shepherd and Blue Heeler were allowed through, but she wasn't. She squealed in protest.

"Oh, Gertie, I won't be long. Chill out," Betty ordered the pig as she latched the chain behind her.

The pot-bellied pig stamped her foot in annoyance.

"Its okay, Gertrude, I promise I won't keep you mum very long and you can come in to visit the next time. I'll even make you a gooey treat of molasses and oats," Rainbow cooed through the wire mesh.

The pig settled down and nosed the young woman who was bending over to talk to her.

Betty shook her head and chuckled.

"You do have a way with animals."

"Thank you," Rainbow said quietly as she stood up, her long dreadlocks swaying gently from side to side.

Blue sprinted ahead of them as they turned to continue their walk up the tree lined drive. The shepherd stayed beside Betty, his right shoulder brushing against her left leg.

"You know you're definitely going to have to adopt Bear," Rainbow chimed, glancing sideways at the older woman.

"Apparently so," Betty agreed.

Since the strange altercation with Barney earlier, Betty had realized that having a canine companion such as the shepherd appeared to be was more than appealing. She couldn't rely on Gertrude to protect her in dangerous situations all the time.

"I might change his name though. He's too handsome for that. Whoever thought naming a drug sniffing dog Bear must have been high themselves."

Rainbow laughed, her eyes sparkling with mirth.

"Actually I'm the only one who calls him Bear. Its short for hug-a-bear because he's such a cuddle-bunny and cuddle-bunny was too feminine. His actual registered name is Brubaker, after Robert Redford's character in the 1980 prison movie."

Betty stopped dead in her tracks. She looked down at the dog that looked expectantly up at her, awaiting her directions, and then burst into a fit of mirth.

The shepherd jumped up and stretched to his full length, placing two paws on her shoulders, his tail snaking happily in the air like a loose garden hose at full tilt.

The Heeler ran in circles around them, barking furiously.

"But he's not even a red head," Betty guffawed.

"No, he's not," Rainbow quipped, before doubling over with laughter.

"Okay, give me the number when we get to your place," Betty said, rubbing the shepherd behind the ears, "but his new name will be Champ. I don't care what it says on his papers."

"Champ it is," Rainbow agreed, rubbing the tears from her eyes. "And I'll call Bob to let him know that a newly retired RCMP sergeant will be calling him."

"Special Consultant to the RCMP Major Crimes Unit actually," Betty corrected the young woman.

"I stand corrected."

They composed themselves and increased their pace up the driveway, the gravel crunching underfoot.

"Bob," Betty queried after a moment, thinking of the dog's name sake.

"Bob," Rainbow acknowledged.

They glanced at each other, and then burst into yet another fit of giggles.

They broke out of the tree lined lane and into the open fields that surrounded the small log home. The Heeler raced into the field chasing after a rabbit, happy to be home.

The newly named shepherd whined, wanting to join the Heeler, but also not wanting to leave its chosen master's side.

Betty thought about telling the dog to go have some fun, but her hackles were up. The bursts of laughter lifted her mood, but there was a dark cloud over the McDonald farm and it wasn't the Cumulonimbus clouds that darkened the sky overhead.

Rainbow was silent too as she climbed the two steps up to the front door of her home. She looked to Betty for reassurance before pushing the door open.

Betty waited outside, hand on her hip, looking for the gun that was no longer there.

"Honey," Betty heard Rainbow call from the kitchen. "Frank, I'm home."

The house was silent.

"He must be in the barn," she said, returning to the front porch.

"Let's go," Betty grimaced, eyeing the barn and the empty patch of earth where the stone angel once stood half way between the barn and the house.

"Where's the angel," Betty asked, pointing towards the black patch of earth beside the fountain. "I hadn't realized it was missing before, although, I should have. It's a huge thing."

"Was that what stood there," Rainbow asked. "I wondered about that. There was nothing here when we came to first view the house and property. I assume the family came and got it, but it was weird as they didn't take any of Summer's belongings. Those are still in the barn."

"Interesting," Betty growled, suspecting she knew who took the angel. Barney had bought it as a gift for Summer when she bought the property after her brother, Moon, managed to squirrel their parent's property out from under her. Everyone on Seal Island knew about it. She suspected that the angel was somewhere on Barney's property.

In truth, Betty was glad it was gone. She could still envision the young hippy girl, eerily similar to the pet psychic walking beside her, lying dead in the arms of the angel, her back shattered from the fall from the barn roof. It was just one more item in the case that she was building on Barney Whyte.

"Heel," Betty commanded the shepherd, even though the dog still stuck to her side like glue.

"Frank," Rainbow called into the barn.

Blue barked and bolted past the two women. The shepherd grumbled, but didn't follow suit.

"Frank," Rainbow called again after receiving no answer.

"That's really odd," the young woman said, turning to Betty. "Let's check the hatchery."

Betty nodded agreement and followed after the woman, still wishing she had a firearm and not just the shepherd at her knee. She also wondered if she shouldn't have let Gertrude come too.

Betty grinned. How many cops could boast that their back-up partners were a dog and pot-bellied pig.

Rainbow swung open the large door into the chick hatchery and peeked inside. She gasped at the stench coming from within.

"What's that smell," Betty asked, covering her nose and mouth.

"It's ammonia. Frank hasn't been cleaning the pens. The chicks are all fine, the heat lamp is on and they still have some dirty water and feed, but the shavings are full of poop," Rainbow grimaced, swinging the door wide open to let in some fresh air. "I have to give them some water at least before we go on and re-fill their feed bin."

Rainbow grabbed a metal bucket from inside the doorway and headed for the outside tap to fill it with water.

Betty looked into the hatchery which had been home to *River's Herbal Home Remedies*. The droning of the peeping chicks was sharp and loud. It hurt her ears. She took a deep breath and walked into the hatchery room.

Cardboard boxes labelled with *River's Herbal Home Remedies* were stacked against one wall. Measuring equipment sat on the counters covered in dust as well as a dozen empty mason jars which weren't so filthy. She recognized those mason jars. They used to hold moonshine.

Betty searched under the table and saw where the empty jars had come from. There were at least a dozen full ones stacked in a plastic milk crate. She slipped her coat sleeve over her hand and examined the empty jars. One of them still held a smidgeon of liquid in it. She pocketed it, careful not to leave any fingerprints on the glass. She then cautiously lifted one of the full jars out of the crate and tucked it inside her lumberjack shirt. It was going to be hard to hide, but she wanted to have it analyzed. The evidence wouldn't stand up in court, but it might provide a lead.

Rainbow returned with a bucket of water.

She pulled open the handmade mesh door to the hatchery and went inside. A hundred little yellow chicks ran over her boots, chirping gleefully. She dumped out what was left of the dirty water in the self-watering container and refilled it.

"Hand me that bag of feed over there will you," Rainbow said, pointing to a twenty pound bag of chick feed slumped against one wall.

Betty hoisted up the bag and handed it over the three foot tall fence surrounding the chick pen all while balancing the full jar and almost empty jars of moonshine cradled under her arm pit beneath her jacket. It was a miracle that she didn't drop one or both of them.

Betty thought she heard the sound of hammering, and then a skill saw, from somewhere at the back of the property. It was hard to tell over the raucous party the chicks were now having.

"You look after the chicks. I'm going to look out back."

"Okay," Rainbow squeaked from behind her.

"Heel, Champ," Betty ordered the shepherd before sauntering off towards the rear of the barn.

She walked by several bird pens. There were two pens with fifty or so pheasants in them and another two pens filled with grouse. All of the pens were unkempt and the birds looked ravenous. Rainbow was going to have her hands full.

She heard a cacophony of barking.

The shepherd at her side whimpered and wagged his tail.

It didn't make her feel better.

She emerged from the back of the barn and saw a bare-chested Frank McDonald putting the finishing touches on what looked like a guillotine. Farther away from the guillotine platform stood a tall pole with chains fastened into a series of large bolts. Bundles of firewood were piled all around the pole.

A guillotine and what looked like a witch burning pyre?

And was that a noose hanging over the big elm tree at the bottom of the meadow?

What was going on?

Frank fired up a battery operated drill and screwed another side brace onto the guillotine's struts. His face and chest dripped with sweat. His muscles bulged.

The shepherd uttered a low growl.

"Yeah, I'm with you there, Champ," she said to the dog.

"Frank, what are you doing," Rainbow yelled, running by Betty.

Betty tried to stop her and instantly regretted it. The mason jar filled with moonshine slipped. It now balanced precariously between her hip and her boob under her lumberjack shirt.

"Honey, what do you think," Rainbow's husband yelled back, his eyes feverish.

"What do I think? I think you've lost your mind," she hollered, anger blazing. "The bird pens haven't been cleaned. The chicks were out of water and almost out of food. The pheasants and grouse are starving."

"That's okay, honey, we're going to let them all go."

"What?"

Betty put a hand around the shepherd's collar as the Heeler ran up to them, tail wagging. Its tail quickly stopped wagging and sank between its back legs when it saw the condition of its master. The dog whined and sat down on the grass behind Betty.

"I told you, babe, I've got the answer to our money problems," Frank gushed, picking up his shirt and wiping his brow.

"What you think we're going to start up a murder farm, like that pig guy in the Fraser Valley," Rainbow snapped.

The look that she gave Betty let Betty know that Rainbow thought her husband had lost his mind too.

"Nothing like that at all, babe. We're going to start a live action role playing murder game. We're going to call it *Murder Most Fowl*. Our motto's going to be: *if you can kill a chicken, you can kill anything*. I got it all figured out," Frank said animatedly, his arms waving about.

"You see," he continued, "it starts with a board game, kind of like *Clue*, only people die by the most gruesome means, some by hanging, others by getting burned alive, and others get their heads whacked off by Madame Guillotine. I'm betting the guillotine will be the most popular. We'll have to have people camp in tents or sleep in the hay-loft until the money starts rolling in, but believe me, it will. Once it does, we'll build some cabins."

"Are you hearing all this," Rainbow asked Betty.

"I am," Betty replied. "I think you better grab some things and I'll take you to stay somewhere else for awhile."

Betty didn't want to mention the judge's name in front of Frank McDonald in the state he was in. Live playing murder games? Who would pay money to do that other than a psychopath? Yet again, she wished that she still had her side arm.

"I can't," Rainbow said. "I can't leave the birds. Look at him. He's insane. He won't look after them."

"He wants you to let them go," Betty answered, "so let them go."

"The chicks are too young. They'll all die."

"I'll go get my dad, Reggie and Morris Tweedsmuir. Morris would be happy to take care of the chicks, I'm sure. He's a good guy. You won't need to worry about them. We'll get Frank some help, I promise."

Rainbow bit her lip, unsure.

Her husband went back to work on the guillotine ignoring his wife and the woman standing behind her.

"You can't stay here," Betty pleaded with Rainbow. "It's not safe."

"I don't know what's wrong with him," she cried, tears streaming down her face. "He's a really nice man. This just isn't him."

"Believe me, I understand more than you know," Betty whispered to the distraught woman.

Rainbow finally nodded and joined Betty on the short walk back to the barn, the dogs clinging to their sides.

"Don't forget, *Murder Most Fowl*, is coming to a farm near you. Tell your friends," Frank McDonald shouted to the backs of the women walking away from him.

Moonshine and Mace

Barney entered the still shed. He had allowed himself to get too carried away in his banter with his best friend's daughter. He didn't know what made him poke the proverbial snake when he made the caustic remarks about that damnable pig of hers and then let fly with a few choice words after the equally damnable German shepherd smelled the drugs on his clothing.

Barney gathered up the tabs of LSD that were strewn about on the bench where several mason jars of moonshine waited to be filled. All of them had smiley faces imprinted on the front of the pills.

He slammed a fist down on the bench.

Smack!

A mason glass fell to the floor and shattered into pieces. Several hits of acid joined them.

"Damn that woman," he exclaimed vehemently.

Camille strolled into the shed, a glass of Chablis in one hand.

"What's going on, my dear," she purred. "We aren't getting shut down, are we? I thought your counteroffer of adding fire extinguishers to the buildings at regular intervals and not hiring anyone under the age of twelve was quite generous."

"No, it's not the problems in India," he growled, bending over to retrieve the hits of acid, pricking his finger on a piece of broken glass.

"Damn it," Barney cursed, removing the sliver of glass from his finger. He grabbed a dirty towel from his work bench and pressed his bloody finger in it until it stopped bleeding.

"What is more important than keeping those rubber factories up and running?"

"Burying the evidence," Barney seethed, throwing the towel on the floor.

"What evidence," Camille asked, puzzled.

"My secret ingredients," Barney continued. "Betty has a drug dog. It sniffed my stash on me. I expect a whole regiment of RCMP officers will show up within the next day or two."

"Shall I get the phone for you," she replied, careful not to frown at the disquieting news less it gives her wrinkles.

"I'll call the lawyers after I'm done," he muttered.

Camille drank her wine while she watched her husband bag up his drugs. After he had all the smiley faced tabs of LSD and a couple ounces of pot bagged up in the green garbage bag, he tossed some loose coffee grains on top of it all to mask the smell. It wasn't a large stash, but it was impressive all the same.

"I'm going to miss our little magic carpet rides in the hot tub," she pouted.

"It won't be for long, sweetie," he said.

Barney marched out of the shed, shovel in hand. He buried his stash inside a deep hole beneath the roots of a large hazel nut tree in the bank above the flower garden, and then dragged some sphagnum moss over the now filled in hole to hide it.

Barney stood back and looked up at the budding tree. He had planted that tree for his wife the day after they got married. She thought it was sweet that he planted a hazelnut tree for Hazel. "A hazel for Hazel," she had said.

Hazel was a sweet woman, a gentle soul who was far too good for him. He regretted the way he had treated her. She was the only one of his wives who had turned down a multi-million-dollar divorce settlement. The piteous look she gave him when she looked at him across the lawyer's desk was worse than the screaming fits and threats of the three wives before her.

"What about the still," Camille asked casually, breaking into Barney's reverie.

Camille stood beside the eight-foot-tall stone angel in whose arms Summer River had let out her last breath.

Barney shivered when he saw Camille standing there. Maybe it hadn't been smart to retrieve that angel from Summer's farm. He only did it because Camille demanded that he do so after he made the mistake of telling her how much he had paid for the thing.

Camille and he started dating about a week before he bought the stone angel for Summer. He felt bad for Summer, losing her fiancé a couple of weeks after losing her parents, and then getting trod on and abused by her idiot brother. It was probably the only gift he had ever bought for a woman that didn't involve sex.

He was still married to Hazel when all this occurred. She had approved of his generosity and had even encouraged it. Hazel married an Anglican Minister about two years after their divorce. Hazel sent him a letter through his lawyer telling him she forgave him. Her generous words cut through his heart like a knife. He married Camille two days later.

Camille was a jealous woman, even if she turned a blind eye to his affairs while they were dating and then again after they were married. She made it clear right from the start: if what he did hurt her in any way, which meant jeopardizing her lifestyle, then she would make him pay.

Barney loved Camille's edge and practiced coolness. He understood Camille. She was a tough cookie. Not much got under her skin. Camille was all about money and the good things in life. They were two peas in a pod in that respect.

Still, as Barney walked over to give his wife a quick peck on the cheek, his eyes were drawn to the upraised arms of the stone angel. For a moment, he thought he saw Summer laying in its arms, facing him, an accusing look on her face.

The shovel clattered out of his hand and Barney clutched his chest. He collapsed to his knees.

"Barney, what's wrong," Camille yelled.

"Call 911," he gasped. "I think I'm having a heart attack."

***

Betty was just getting Summer settled in at Violet Bone's house when her cell phone rang. She was surprised to see Tom Powder's name on the screen. It was almost as if he'd read her mind.

"I was just going to call you," Betty said after she picked up the call.

Betty stepped out onto the porch, looking for some privacy.

Sir Percival, a former barn cat with the attitude to go with it, hissed at the little blue, grey and black Heeler from his perch on a lounge chair cushion. The Heeler yawned and raised a paw in an offering of friendship, but the cat was having none of it.

Champ, her new partner, lay in the grass chewing happily on a stick.

Gertrude and Peaches were getting into trouble in the garden. They exposed roots. They tossed aside plants. Gertrude was happy doing what she did best–creating havoc, while Peaches munched away on an early crop of tulips.

Vi and Rainbow were making tea in the kitchen.

Betty closed the door behind her so that the two women wouldn't hear her conversation. She would probably tell Vi about it later but didn't want to talk in front of Rainbow. Rainbow had enough to worry about.

"Barney had a heart attack," she gasped, shocked at the news that Tom had just shared. "When?"

Betty listened to Tom's account.

"That's good timing then, not the heart attack I suppose, but it goes to the reason that I was going to call you."

Betty filled Tom in on her odd conversation with Barney as well as details on her new partner, a police force certified drug sniffing German shepherd and the dog's reaction to Barney.

"And I also need you to run a test on the moonshine I removed from Frank and Rainbow McDonald's farm. I told Rainbow what I found. She told me that Barney had brought a couple of mason jars over as a house warming gift, but that they were still under the kitchen sink, so the jars I found in the barn were from there before they bought the property. She gave me permission, after the fact, I admit, to removing the jars and submitting them for testing given her husband's recent behaviour."

Betty felt a weightlifting off her shoulders when Tom told her he'd organize a team.

"And Tom," she continued after he finished talking, "I may need a second med vac for Frank McDonald. I suspect that the LSD that was in Andy's system may have come from Barney's moonshine. Frank is out-there, and I mean out-there. He's building a hit man's paradise in his back yard, complete with a working guillotine. There are empty moonshine jars everywhere in the chick hatchery in the barn. I grabbed one of the empty ones so you can test that too. I will jump on a float plane and bring them over to you. I'll text you when we're landing."

Betty waited for his confirmation on time frame and then hung up the phone.

She turned to see both Judge Bone and Vi standing in the open doorway behind her. She was so engrossed in her conversation with Inspector Powder that she didn't hear them open the door. Betty judged from their expressions they had heard almost every word.

"Oh my God, you think Frank is high," Rainbow trembled.

"We won't know until we get the results back, but yes, I believe he is," Betty said.

"And he has no idea that he might be ingesting contaminated moonshine," Vi added.

"That is correct," Betty agreed.

"And you think that's what sent Andy into a sudden rage? LSD laced moonshine?" Vi finished.

"Correct again," Betty nodded, "but without doing blood tests on Frank and toxicology screening on the old moonshine in your barn, Rainbow, we can't be sure. That alone should give us enough for a warrant, but I think Champ's signalling to a bonafide Special Consultant to the RCMP Major Crimes Unit that Barney Whyte was positive for drugs should tip the scale."

"How do I get Frank to agree to the blood tests," Rainbow asked. "He hates needles and in the state that he is in, he won't agree to it."

"We'll tell him he has bird flu," Betty said after a moment.

"What if it doesn't work," worried Rainbow.

"Then I'll provoke him into attacking me, so I have to mace him."

"You are devious, retired Sergeant Betty Bruce," Vi said. The old judge then broke into a wide grin.

"Sometimes I scare even myself," Betty returned.

"What's your plan now," Vi asked innocently.

"To hop on a float plane, of course."

"Who will watch the property in case Barney burns the place down and makes a run for it back to the States," Vi cautioned her friend.

Betty sighed heavily.

"Barney's had a heart attack," Betty sighed. "He's been taken by helicopter to the hospital in Vancouver."

"Oh, my goodness," Vi exclaimed.

"That's horrible," Rainbow gasped. "And we just saw him this morning."

"I'll make it a round trip and be back as fast as I can. I can't stop Camille from setting fire to the place if she is home and so chooses, but I can get that warrant happening as soon as possible," she glowered.

"What about me," Rainbow queried. "What can I do to help?"

Judge Bone turned to the younger woman. She grinned, and then walked into the office, returning with a bible in her hand.

"Put your left hand on the bible and raise your right hand," the judge ordered the pet psychic.

Rainbow did as she was told.

"Do you so swear on this bible and in front of an officer of the court that you gave retired Sergeant Beatrice Bruce permission to remove two mason jars, one that was empty, and one that was full, from the barn on your property," the judge purred.

"I do," Rainbow replied, mildly puzzled.

"And are the two mason jars sitting on my table in the kitchen, the two mason jars that you gave retired Sergeant Bruce permission to remove from the property," Vi continued.

"I guess so," Rainbow said.

"Yes or no please," Vi asked the blushing woman.

"Yes," Rainbow said with finality. "Betty showed them to me and asked permission to take them, which I gave her."

The three women smiled at each other.

"Off you go, Bet," Vi ordered her friend. "I'll look after getting Gertrude and Peaches back to your father and prepare an affidavit for the chain of custody for Rainbow to sign. I can witness it."

"Okay, but not a word to him about this to anyone, including my father, and Rainbow, keep out of sight. No going out into the garden. Keep Blue and Champ in the back and away from the road."

"Okay," Rainbow agreed.

"And Vi, don't let my dad come over here for two days. He doesn't know about any of this and I want to keep it that way, otherwise everyone on the island will know what's happening. He just can't help himself," Betty cautioned the judge.

"That is true. Your father is a bit of a gossip," Vi mused. "Well, it's a pact then, as they like to say on TV."

The three-women fist bumped each other: they made the pact.

"Wait a minute, what about the birds," Rainbow trembled. "You said that we can ask the Old Spice guy, and someone named Morris to help?"

"I forgot about your chicks," Betty confessed.

"What chicks," Vi questioned the two.

"Rainbow's husband isn't looking after the birds."

"I fed and watered them all before we left, but their pens are filthy and the feed won't last for long," Rainbow cried. "I can't leave them."

"I'll only be a few hours, Rainbow," Betty consoled the young woman. "I'll go over to Reggie's as soon as I get back and we'll fetch Morris. I don't think we can take all the birds, but we can definitely round up the chicks."

"They are the ones who need help the most," she replied, calming down. "Frank said to release the grouse and pheasants, so go for it."

"Are you sure," Betty asked shakily. The islander's reaction to a hundred plus pheasants and grouse being let loose on the island all at once would be frightening. It would be like the Wild West.

Lord knows who might get shot in the process. She didn't have the heart to tell Rainbow that most of them would end up on someone's dinner plate.

"Yes, I'm sure," Rainbow said with resolution.

"All right then, Betty Bruce, bird wrangler, at your service," Betty quipped.

Pipe Dreams

Betty pulled up in front of the docks in her father's pickup truck. She hated lying to him, but she couldn't tell him where she was going or what she was going to do without revealing Rainbow's plight.

She had thrown an old dog crate that she found in her barn and several cardboards boxes that she had saved from her move into the back of the truck.

Night was falling and there wasn't much time, so she knew she had to work fast. The float plane trip had proven bumpy but uneventful. She hated to turn Tom's dinner invitation down, but she promised Rainbow she'd rescue the chicks tonight.

She walked down to the docks, heading for *The Persephone*. She had to admit that the reconditioned wooden trawler was beautiful with its black paint, red trim, and polished aged deck. Reggie had done a wonderful job renovating the old girl.

Betty jumped over the rail and knocked on the bridge's door. No one answered.

She tried the handle, and it was open.

"Reggie," she called, pushing the door open.

She knew Reggie liked to sleep in the trawler after he'd had a few pints at the pub, and sometimes 'just because'. The trawler had been his home at sea for over thirty years.

When Reggie didn't answer her call, she realized with an inward groan that he might still be at the pub. She hadn't wanted to go in there as questions would abound after she was seen flying away in a float plane one minute and returning an hour and a half later.

She walked spread-legged across the rolling dock as the wind picked up from the northeast. It was a bitter wind. She shivered and tugged up her coat collar. She couldn't wait for summer.

A quick check at the pub revealed that the Old Spice guy, as Rainbow called him, wasn't there either. She only popped in for a few seconds, but even then, questions were shouted out: how was Barney and where did she go in such a hurry? Ugh, small islands.

Betty climbed back into the pick-up truck and drove up South Shore Road, heading towards Reggie's farm.

Betty hadn't been to Reggie's farm for a few years, not since she helped him go legit with a government issued medical marijuana grow license. He'd been growing and distributing pot for years since the fishing industry tanked, but she left him alone as he was a small fry in the grand scheme of things, and she'd known him all her life. He was a few years ahead of her in school. She remembered him as a tall gangly island kid who didn't take guff from anyone and stood up for the underdog. He left school at seventeen to go to work on his father's trawler and never came back.

Betty wasn't prepared for the spectacle that greeted her when she drove into the yard.

Eight long greenhouses lined either side of the drive. A new building had been erected in what used to be an apple orchard. She assumed the new structure was a lab. White lab coats ruled as studious technicians bent over microscopes while others cared for the budding plants. Blue and red heat lamps created eerie shadows in the greenhouses.

There was also what looked to be a bunk house at the back of the property behind Reggie's one-bedroom cabin.

She pulled up in front of the cabin. There was movement behind the curtain in the living room.

Betty parked the truck and headed for the front door.

Before she could knock, Reggie opened the door, coffee cup in hand. His face lit up like the northern lights when he saw who was standing there.

"While, Bet, this is a pleasure," he drawled.

"Reggie," Betty gasped, shocked. "You look so different."

This was a Reggie that Betty hadn't met before. Gone were the black gumboots, ivory wool fisherman's sweater and grey toque.

Instead, the broad-shouldered fisherman dressed in pale blue jeans, a navy-blue turtleneck, and a white lab coat, all of which highlighted the white in his grey hair and deepened the blue in his glacier blue eyes.

"That's 'cause these here are my work clothes," he blushed. "I'd rather be fishing, but ya gotta do what ya gotta do these days."

"That's true," Betty replied, feeling like she needed to push her jaw, which had dropped open unbecomingly, back into place.

"I was just headin' ta the lab, you want ta join me," Reggie asked her. "Oh, jumpin' jiminy, where's my manners? Would ya like a coffee, Bet. I got a fresh pot on the stove. It's real coffee, not that bullshite blend that the kids in the lab like."

Betty laughed. She agreed with him. She didn't like the 'bullshite blends' either.

"Normally, I'd say that I'd love one, but like always, I need some help with a very delicate matter and you're the only man on this island I trust, Reggie," she stammered, feeling awkward under her friend's intense gaze.

"Ya know ya can always count on me," he said huskily.

Betty felt herself flushing.

"I do, Reg," she stuttered.

"Ya got time ta look in on the kids with me afore we go dealing with that delicate matter," he asked her.

"Can't see the harm in it," she replied. "We're going to go rescue some chicks from the McDonald farm. I thought we could stop at Morris' farm to see if he can take them. There are about a hundred of the little bundles of sunshine."

Reggie burst out laughing, a booming sound that Santa would have been proud of. His eyes twinkled with delight.

"Ah, Bets, the things ya get yerself into," he guffawed. "I won't ask why we're rescuing a bunch of baby chicks. I'm sure you'll tell me when yer ready, but we don't have to take 'em to Morris'. We can bring them 'ere. Come on, the kids in the lab will love this."

Betty followed the sizeable man into the lab.

Betty didn't think she could be more surprised than she was, but the sight of all the young twenty-somethings working studiously under the glare of the fluorescent lights, a radio blaring out country tunes in the background was not something she saw every day. Two girls and one of the boys had long dread-locked hair just like Rainbow's, while several other of the men sported cowboy boots under their Mr. Clean lab attire.

Reggie smiled at the look of awe and delight on Betty's face.

"Ain't it something," he whispered, amused. "They're really good kids too. They got an agreement. They listen ta an hour of country and then switch ta an hour of this awful reggae stuff. Although, I'm kinda gettin' used ta it."

"Reggie, I'm sorry but I've got to ask you. Please tell me this is all legal," she whispered back.

Reggie chuckled, his shoulders rolling with mirth.

"Ah, Bets, yer so funny. Course its legal. I got a contract with Grasshopper Corp. I gotta knack for growing, always have. Get it from my ma."

Reggie escorted her forward along the rows of research stations. The 'kids' as Reggie called the lab techs nodded a hello as they walked by.

"See here," Reggie continued, "I've been developin' these new strains of pot and I sold the rights ta Grasshopper. I've got Penny Lane which is really mellow and is fer folks that suffer from depression, and then there's Diamond Lucy, the Yellow Submarine and Jude. The Yellow Submarine's more potent than Barney's moonshine... which I never touch, by the way. That stuff'll make ya crazy. Yellow Submarine is fer cancer patients ta help em with the pain. As ya can tell, I've always had a thing for the Beatles. Grasshopper doesn't call 'em by that name cause of copyright and stuff, but I do."

It dumbfounded Betty. She had been so consumed with her own matters that she never knew what one of her oldest and dearest friends was up to. She was embarrassed. How could she be so blind? And how come nobody ever told her about it at the pub? Was everyone that intimidated by her?

"Hey, young 'uns," Reggie called out.

The group of young technicians wordlessly looked up.

"We gotta help a fellow islander out. My friend Betty here and me are gonna go pick us up about a hundred little chicks that need some nurturing so I need you guys ta fix up a section of the back of the lab with some chicken wire I got around back of number eight and a couple of heat lamps. If'n we don't keep the chicks warm; they huddle all on top of each other and the ones underneath, they get smothered. It's a terrible sight, I can tell ya," Reggie said with a shake of his grey and white mane of hair.

The lab techs all broke into a series of grins with a few shouts of 'awesome' and 'all right'. In a flurry of white coats, they dropped what they were doing and scuttled off to build a chick pen.

"I don't know what to say," Betty croaked, tears forming in her eyes.

"Ya don't gotta say nothing," Reggie murmured. "Let's go get those hundred yellow bundles of sunshine, as you call 'em."

**

It was dark by the time that Betty and Reggie pulled into the McDonald farmyard. The house was dark, but lights blazed in the barn.

"This ain't right," Reggie muttered as he got out of Betty's truck.

"What do you know about Barney and his moonshine," Betty whispered as she rounded the front of the truck?

"I know it can make people crazy," Reggie ventured. "I've seen it one too many times. It's why I don't touch the stuff. You shouldn't either."

"I've had it a few times, but mostly a half shot in my coffee. It's got a bite, that's for sure, but it did nothing but help me wake up. Maybe I should have asked you about it before."

"You said in the truck that Frank's been inta'it," he asked her.

"Yeah, there's a whole crate of it in the barn. Rainbow told me it must have been there when they bought the place as she'd never seen it before until I pointed it out before we left this afternoon."

Reggie grunted in response.

Betty wondered how much the old fisherman knew about Barney's Brew.

They walked slowly towards the barn, trying to be as quiet as possible. Betty had warned Reggie that she didn't know what kind of state Frank after what might be in she witnessed in the afternoon. To say it was alarming was an understatement. Once again, she wished she had a badge and a gun. She wondered too if she should have brought Champ for back-up.

"Why don't ya let me go in first," Reggie offered as they crept toward the open barn door. "Frank knows me. I helped them move their furniture in."

"That was mighty good of you," Betty whispered.

"It's what neighbours are for," he whispered back.

"Okay, but I'm going to be right behind you."

Reggie grinned and gave her a thumbs-up.

Betty watched Reggie enter the barn. His broad shoulders blocked out the light and plunged her world into darkness. She felt her stomach flip-flop. Bile rose into her throat. This was a foolish idea, rescuing chicks by the dark of night.

She inched slowly around the doorway, picking up a shovel that was leaning against the wall as she did so.

The barn smelled like ammonia from the dirty bird pens. Pigeons cooed in the rafters. Pheasants and grouse huddled inside their respective pens. They were all deathly quiet. Betty hoped that they weren't dead.

Reggie disappeared into the chick hatchery.

She waited, holding the shovel like a bat.

"S'okay," he boomed, sticking his head out of the hatchery door and beckoning her inside. "He's out cold."

Betty put down the shovel. She peeked inside the hatchery. Frank sat on a stool, slumped over a bench, two empty bottles of moonshine beside him, his face and t-shirt sweat stained, his coveralls black at the knees.

"Remind's me of my old man. He used ta drink himself into a stupor like that," Reggie grumbled. "Stupid thing ta do. He won't come round fer hours. Why don't ya go fetch yer truck and I'll start gathering up these poor little tykes?"

"I didn't know your father drank," she replied softly, not as confident as Reggie that the fellow snoring loudly in the corner wouldn't wake up and attack them.

"He didn't drink like this 'ere fellow until he retired. When the boom was over and it was clear fishing wasn't ever gonna recover, my old man lost it," Reggie confided. "That's why I like a few beers, but mostly stick ta weed. Ya don't get mean on my weed."

"I'm so sorry," Betty gasped, finding a new respect for the man standing before her looking down with pity on the farmer who wanted to start up a murder enterprise.

"Go get the truck, Bets," Reggie ordered her gently.

Betty turned to go.

"Oye, Bets, what are we gonna do with all the other birds? We can't leave 'em," Reggie asked.

"Rainbow said to release them," she grimaced.

Reggie chuckled.

"Freedom it is," he chortled.

Betty retrieved the truck while Reggie set about opening all the doors to the pheasant and grouse cages.

She parked the truck right in front of the barn doors. Betty was just about to grab the dog crate out of the truck bed when a bevy of fowl burst out of the open door, some in flight and some at the run, feathers flapping, as a broomstick wielding ragtag of a fishermen slash pot grower scooted the birds out the doorway, his white lab coat billowing out behind him like angel's wings.

In silhouette, with the lit barn at his back, her friend did indeed look like the archangel Gabriel.

Betty and Reggie worked studiously, dodging this way and that, corralling the chicks into the dog crate and cardboard boxes, while Frank McDonald slept on.

The chicks were more slippery and fast than Betty expected. They cheeped and chirped and raced under her feet. She and Reggie twisted themselves into pretzels, trying to catch them all.

Betty and Reggie dripped with sweat. They high fived each other for a job well done after they put the last chick inside the box.

"Ya know, I think we should organize what-do-ya-call one of them things... an intervention, that's it, for Frank," Reggie suggested as he punched a few holes in the top of the boxes with a pocket knife so that the chicks could breathe.

"I've got that all arranged," Betty replied.

Reggie nodded in acknowledgement. His gruff exterior softened as he looked over the six cardboard boxes and one dog crate full of chirping chicks.

"It's a good thing we're doing," he mumbled.

"I couldn't have done it without you," Betty agreed.

"Nope, you couldn't," he answered slowly before breaking into a toothy grin. "T'was sure amusing ta watch ya chase those little chickies around."

Betty slapped him playfully on the arm.

"Come on, Sir Reginald, it's time to get going," she giggled.

"Don't run into those birds on the way out," Reggie guffawed, pointing to the pheasant strolling across the driveway in front of the truck. "They're thick as fence posts."

Betty choked on a laugh as she climbed into the pickup truck. She had needed a good dose of Reggie Phoenix. He always made her day a bit brighter.

Reggie climbed into the passenger seat, a crooked smile on his face.

Betty glanced his way as she drove cautiously up the drive, several times having to swerve around a pack of pheasants who mulled about, too dumb struck to realize that they were free. Reggie's profile was strong, his beard neatly trimmed, his nose slightly upturned, and his steely gaze fixed out the window. There was a lot more depth to Reggie Phoenix that she had ever imagined.

Huh! Who knew?

Betty smiled and then slammed on the brakes as a covey of grouse flew across the front of the truck, heading for the fields of heather in the far reaches of the farm.

Hazel's Revenge

Forty-eight hours after Betty arrived in Vancouver by float plane with the two mason jars, properly bagged and tagged, and had handed them off to Tom Powder, Doc Forester had the results and the search warrant was issued. The empty mason jar tested positive for trace amounts of LSD, and the full mason jar was lethal, according to Forester.

Betty had kept a watchful eye on Barney's property until the team was ready to descend upon Seal Island once more, even though Tom had told her that Barney had been medi-evacuated out by helicopter. Camille apparently had stayed behind, and Betty had seen her out wandering the garden many times.

Betty met the long line of police vehicles and forensic vans at the front gate to Barney and Camille Whyte's property six hours after the search warrant had been issued, the German shepherd formerly named Brubaker standing at attention beside her. The German shepherd puffed out his chest and whined with glee when the convoy arrived.

"No getting over-excited or cowering at all the people, Champ," she cautioned the dog. "We've got work to do. No distractions. You hear me?"

The dog licked her hand.

Betty smiled, confident in her new partner.

Rainbow had called Bob, the head of the security team at the airport, the next morning after Betty and Reggie had liberated Rainbow's birds.

Bob was brisk and official, but when Betty told him of Brubaker's successful involvement in a drug and active murder investigation on Seal Island, he softened quickly. Once Bob realized who

Betty was, the police sergeant who was directly responsible for solving the case of the severed feet in sneakers, he approved her adoption of the shepherd right away, promising to rubber stamp the papers and email them to her for confirmation within the hour. To say he was thrilled at the prospect of his 'almost' namesake partnering up with a semi-retired RCMP sergeant and special consultant to the Major Crimes Unit, was an understatement. Betty hung up the phone with the promise that the next time she was in Vancouver, she would stop by the airport with Brubaker, now named 'Champ', for a visit.

Betty looked down with affection at her new partner. She straightened her back and proudly prepared to bust Barney and Camille Whyte for illegal alcohol manufacturing and sales, possession of an illegal substance, and drug dealing, even though Barney was currently on the mainland undergoing emergency quadruple by-pass surgery.

The lead unmarked police vehicle, a dark blue SUV, stopped in front of her. The window rolled down.

"Beeetttty," the handsome Native inspector crooned, his eyes sparkling, "we have to stop meeting like this."

Betty felt her knees go weak. Tom Powder was a handsome man with salt and pepper blue-black hair, dark brown eyes, coffee cream skin and an abundance of laugh lines. It was the laugh lines and labyrinthine eyes that made her heart pump, although she also thought of Reggie Phoenix in his navy-blue turtleneck and snow-white lab coat.

Maybe she was over-tired, she reasoned, or just pumped up with too much adrenaline.

"Fancy meeting you here, Tom," she joked.

"What do I call you now that you're retired," Tom's arrogant partner, Inspector Ben Hammerton, asked from the driver's seat.

"You can call me Special Agent or Miss Bruce," Betty remarked snidely. The younger detective's good looks would make Adonis jealous. They got off on the wrong foot when they first met after he tasered Peaches. It was all she could do to keep him from getting lynched by the irate mob in front of the pub. Betty knew that despite what Powder said about his being a talented detective, she would never like him.

"I called ahead. The wife is home," Tom added, wagging a finger in warning at Betty for her pointed sense of humour.

"True love is made of money, it seems," Betty grinned, unable to help herself.

"And who's this fine specimen of a dog standing beside you," Powder asked, admiring the beautiful shepherd.

"This is Champ, my new partner," Betty replied, introducing the dog.

Champ wagged his tail, his eyes examining the inspector with interest.

"I read your report. He's a drug sniffer, isn't he," Hammerton asked.

"He is," Betty nodded. "When Mr. Whyte came to the fence to speak to me two days ago, Champ gave the signal that he smelled drugs on him."

"Let's hope he can do that today too," Hammerton growled.

"He will. I'm sure of that," Betty remarked, a hint of reproach in her voice.

"You want to let us in then," the young inspector said insolently.

Tom rolled his eyes at Betty. Betty grinned.

Betty opened the gate and the eight vehicles rolled in. Champ barked excitedly as each one passed.

"Good dog," Betty said to her partner. "Let's wipe the smirk right off that jerk's face."

Betty waved at Corporal Singh and Doc Forester as they drove past her. The driveway was too short for all the vehicles, so Betty told the other drivers to park on the road.

Betty walked up the lane to Barney's house as two of the police officers cordoned off the front gate with police tape to keep any curious onlookers out.

Neither Betty nor the police officers counted on Gertrude, though.

***

Betty and Champ followed Tom Powder, Ben Hammerton, and Doc Forester into the shed where Barney kept his still while Corporal Singh served the search warrant on Camille Whyte.

Tom Powder whistled in appreciation at the size of the still and the woodpile on the far wall.

"Now that is impressive," Hammerton piped in.

About twenty crates full of mason jars filled to the brim with moonshine were stacked neatly beside the bags of grain and hops. There was also a full gallon of moonshine in a bucket beneath the copper drain waiting to be bottled.

Betty had never been to Barney's home, even in all the years he had been a friend to her father. She'd had a lot of shocks in the past few days, and this one was in the top three.

Powder, Hammerton, and Doc Forester all donned latex gloves. Betty and her dog waited at the door until they were invited in.

"That looks like old solder on those pipes on the still," Doc Forester quipped, pointing to the still's piping. "I was only looking for drugs in the brief analysis of the moonshine sample you brought in Betty. I'm going to call the lab and have them re-test for lead."

"You think that might be the source of McDowell's lead poisoning," Tom asked the coroner.

"It might account for some, but not all," he replied. "I firmly believe that most it was in the old pipes removed from his house during the renovation, but it's too late to test for that."

The statement stunned Betty.

Hammerton walked over to the jug of newly brewed moonshine and took a sniff.

"Wowsers, that is some powerful stuff," the detective cried out, turning his head away. He wiped his watery eyes with a shirt sleeve.

"Looks like some bits of broken glass on the floor over here," Forester mused, kneeling to look at the bits of broken glass from the jar that Barney broke.

"And a bloody rag over there," Betty pointed to a stained rag that had been kicked under a bench.

"So it is," the coroner said, standing up. His knees popped and creaked as he did so. "Darn this getting old."

"I'm thinking, Doc, that after what I read in Summer's diary, that maybe you should compare the DNA in that bloody rag to Summer's baby," Betty croaked, still unable to believe that Summer would have an affair with Barney, yet it seemed the more plausible choice, given Summer didn't directly identify the baby's father in any of the pages that Betty had read.

"You really think he might have killed Summer," Tom asked, his brows furrowed.

"I think if Barney had a kid at this late stage of the game, he's got a whole parcel of wives with a motive to make sure that baby was never born," Betty said ruefully.

"Including the current missus," Hammerton turned towards her, his tone a lot more respectful than he'd ever been.

At that moment, the current missus already a bit tipsy strode across the yard and burst into the shed.

"I've called our lawyers," she screamed, her eyes ablaze with anger.

Betty felt the daggers sinking into her chest when Camille rounded on her, her normally stoic composure completely gone.

"This is your fault. You just couldn't leave us alone," Camille wailed at Betty.

Champ growled and barked furiously at the irate woman, but Camille was in such a rage, she ignored the shepherd completely.

Betty kept a tight hold on Champ. The last thing she wanted was him biting the distressed and angry woman, even though Betty wouldn't mind taking a bite out of her as well.

"Officers," Tom Powder called in the back-up, "get this woman out of here."

"They have a legal right to be here, Camille. Corporal Singh served you the warrant," Betty tried to placate Barney's wife over the barking of the shepherd.

"I don't care about your warrant. I'm an American citizen. Our lawyers are already working at having it thrown out," Camille spat, digging the imaginary knife deeper into Betty's chest. "You aren't a cop anymore and you have been harassing us."

"What," Betty gasped. "Harassing you? How?"

Inspector Powder planted himself between Betty, her dog, and the billionaire's wife.

"Miss Bruce is a Special Consultant to the RCMP," Powder said as two of his men grabbed Camille gently by the arm. "She has every right to be here."

"As far as I'm concerned, I did not give you permission to be here and your warrant is a farce," Camille sputtered, pulling her arms out of the officer's grasp.

"This is an ongoing drug and alcohol investigation," Hammerton growled, walking forward to stand by his partner. "And as we've said, Miss Bruce is a member of our team. She has every right to be here as does the canine officer."

Betty was flummoxed. Inspector Hammerton had just stood up for her and the shepherd.

Behind them, Doc Forester bagged and tagged the bloody rag and then swept up the pieces of glass he'd found on the floor.

"You can't take that... that stuff," Camille continued to rage, noticing the evidence that the coroner was gathering. "And those people in my house can't take anything either. I forbid it."

"Good for you, lady," Hammerton regaled the woman, "forbid away. We can add obstruction of a police officer in the performance of his duties to the charges."

For the first time, Betty felt an inkling of respect for the young man.

"Why don't you go in the house and have a drink, Camille. I'm sure you've a bottle or two of wine open," Betty suggested, slinging some of her own daggers.

Camille glared at the taciturn woman standing shoulder-to-shoulder between two rather large and determined police detectives with a now calmer German shepherd at her side.

"Tell me, Camille, why aren't you at your husband's bedside," Betty continued. "Quadruple bi-pass is major surgery. Aren't you afraid for Barney?"

Camille flipped Betty the bird and twirled on her high heels, which wasn't an easy feat on the gravel walkway that led from the shed to the house.

"Meow," Tom teased her after Camille stalked off.

Betty rolled her eyes at him.

Tom motioned for the two officers to follow the retreating woman back to the house.

Doc Forester finished sweeping the bits of broken glass into an evidence bag.

"All right, Betty, let's see what your partner can uncover," Doc Forester said, eyeing the shepherd.

"Okay, Champ, time to strut your stuff," Betty whispered in the dog's ear.

The dog whined and wagged its tail, happy to be working beside his new handler.

Betty let out the leash and let the shepherd go to work. As soon as she walked over to the place where the broken glass had been beside the still, he lay down and looked at her.

"You guys see anything," she asked the men. "He's clearly signaling that there were drugs here."

The men searched the shed, looking for powder or tabs of acid.

"Maybe whatever was in the smashed jar was laced with LSD," Forrester suggested.

"Could be, given what you told me," Betty agreed.

Betty rubbed Chance's head and pulled him away from the floor where the jar had broken.

"Search," Betty commanded the dog.

The dog sniffed and sniffed. He stopped and lied down at two more places, once beside a bench and the second time by a tray of lemons and oranges.

Betty was about to move the tray when Tom stopped her.

"This is where I take over," he said.

Tom moved the whicker tray of fruit and found a tab of acid stuck to its underside.

"Good dog," Betty rewarded the dog.

The shepherd yawned and wagged its tail.

Betty chuckled.

"Not much of a drug stash," Hammerton whined.

"Wait until we test all those bottles of moonshine," Forester added.

All at once there was a loud crash and a series of shouts.

"LOOK OUT," an officer by the gate yelled.

"GRAB HER," yelled another officer.

"BETTY, GERTRUDE'S ON THE LOOSE," Corporal Singh screamed from the rear of the house.

"Oh, no," Betty gulped, rushing out of the shed.

Betty slid on the gravel, almost tumbling backwards over the shepherd, as her pot-bellied pig ran by, stubby legs barely able to carry the rotund body as the flesh on its tummy wobbled back and forth.

"Gertrude, you stop right now," Betty bellowed.

The pig ignored her and played dodge-the-pig with the four officers chasing her.

"Don't even think of pulling out a taser," Tom warned his partner.

"Fine, but can I shoot it instead," Hammerton muttered back.

"Oh, hold on to Champ, will you," Betty tossed the end of the leash to Tom, not bothering to wait for a reply.

Gertrude ran through the garden, down the stairs to the beach, back up to the house, around the stone angel that Betty at once recognized as the one from Summer's property, and then into the cultured forest whereupon she suddenly ground to a halt, nose to the ground.

Betty and the officers chasing the pig came to a halt as well.

"Okay, guys, let me handle this," Betty gasped, breathless.

The officers backed off, pleased to let Betty take over.

Camille chose that moment to fling off her shoes and race towards the pig, high heels in hand, the pointed part aimed downwards like a pickaxe.

"Stop her," Betty yelled to the officers.

The largest of the officers grabbed the crazy woman around the waist and flung her backwards to the ground. Two officers raced in and subdued her, leaving the third to cuff her hands behind her back, all while the lovely trophy wife screamed some very unlady-like curses their way.

Betty turned around to see Gertrude digging furiously at the base of a hazel tree.

"What's she doing," Powder asked, joining Betty.

Champ barked and leapt forward, pulling the leash out of Tom's grasp. The shepherd ran to Betty and nosed her hand. Betty absently stroked his head while her pig continued to dig up the roots of the hazel tree.

"Truffles," Betty sighed.

"Truffles," Tom queried.

"You know those stinky black things that all the French restaurants shave onto everything," Ben said, joining the other two.

Champ started barking when Gertrude pulled a plastic bag out of the soil. He lunged forward.

"Champ," Betty yelled. "Come."

The dog jumped onto the plastic bag before Gertrude shredded it and lied down on top of it. He growled at the pig, more in warning than to get in a fight with her.

Gertrude snorted snot all over the dog and then resumed rummaging under the tree. She came up with a walnut sized black truffle in her mouth and then waddled away.

"No," Camille screamed. "That's our cat. Get the dog off our cat. Your pig just dug up Fluffy."

"You don't have a cat, Camille, you hate them. I remember you telling Vi to keep Percy away from you, Betty drawled.

Camille sat on the ground, hands cuffed behind her back, sulking.

Hammerton wandered over and retrieved the green garbage bag from under the shepherd. Champ whined and salivated. The young inspector opened the bag to reveal Barney's stash of drugs.

"I think the pig might be a drug sniffer too," Hammerton casually remarked.

Everyone except for Camille burst out laughing.

"That's not ours and you can't prove it," Camille whimpered.

"If Barney's fingerprints are on it, it will," Betty admonished the woman. "Maybe yours are too!"

An officer pulled Camille to her feet. He was about to lead the disheveled woman away when Betty put up a hand to stop him.

"So, Camille, did you know that Barney was about to become a father," Betty asked her.

"What if I did," she muttered, her eyes glittering like a cat stalking its prey. "Why would I care if he fathered a brat with some hippy chic?"

"How did you know it was Summer that I was talking about," Betty asked, her eyes narrowing to thing slits as she unsuccessfully tried to hide her anger.

"It's a great motive for murder, Mrs. Whyte," Tom added.

"Get me out of here," Camille growled, spinning around. She staggered as her nylon clad feet spun on the loose gravel. The officer holding her right arm steadied her and led her towards the police cruiser, parked in the drive.

"Does Barney know that you murdered his baby," Betty called out, bending over to pick Camille's high-heeled shoes out of the dirt.

"Of course, he does. He didn't want the brat either," she screamed.

Camille blanched, realizing that Betty had just tricked her into admitting to murder.

"Hang on, I want to read the lady her Miranda rights," Tom bellowed, striding across the garden.

"Sorry you can't do it, Special Agent Bruce," Hammerton joked as he sauntered by Betty, the plastic bag full of drugs in one hand. "Nicely done."

"Just so long as justice is done, Adonis," she joked back.

The inspector laughed and flipped Betty the bird.

Betty flipped it right back.

One bizarre death solved, two more to go, Betty thought as she bent down on one knee and gave her dog an enormous hug.

"Let's go gather up Gertie before someone turns her into bacon, shall we," she said to the German shepherd.

Too late she noticed that Gertrude had finished her rotting

truffle and was barreling back to search for more.

Betty let go of the shepherd's leash and dove on top of the pig, trying to stop it from doing anymore damage, just as her father ducked under the police tape.

Archie strode towards his daughter as several officers raced to stop him. One of them grabbed him none too gently.

"Unhand me," he demanded, his face blazing with anger.

"Let him go, I need some help here," Betty shouted, seeing her father bunch up his fists. That was all she needed.

The officer muttered an apology as he let the old man go.

Betty straddled Gertrude, feeling like a six-year-old kid trying to ride a sheep in a mutton race, as the pig buried her snout in the black earth around the tree roots, looking for more rotting truffles. Normally, truffles were found in the fall, but somehow the pig had found some old ones that hadn't decayed into the soil yet.

"Why did it take a phone call from Stew to know that my best buddy's house was being searched while he was undergoing major surgery," her father seethed.

"Not now, Dad," Betty countered.

"Yes, now," Archie demanded.

"Damn it, Pops, we have to get Gertrude out of here, she's destroying a crime scene," Betty shouted, noticing that Doc Forester, the forensic crew and half a dozen police officers were watching them, wide grins on their normally stern faces. She even swore that her dog was grinning at her as she wrestled with the pig.

Archie stood with his hands on his hips, refusing to budge.

"I can't comment on active investigations and you know it," she grumbled.

Archie sighed and walked up to Gertrude. He lifted her muddy snout and looked her in the eye.

"Time to go home, Gert," he whispered.

The pig nosed his chin, leaving a black streak of dirt across his day-old growth of beard.

"Come on then, Gert, we're not wanted here. Let's go have tea and biscuits and watch the game," Archie said, grabbing the pig by the ear. "On second thoughts, let's crack open a couple of beers."

Betty slipped off the pot-bellied pig onto the ground and sat there, shoulders slumped, her legs splayed out. Her dog raced over and lied down beside her. The shepherd rested its head in her lap.

"Camille just confessed to murdering Summer, Pops," she breathed, stroking the dog's head.

Her father stared down at her; his face filled with conflicting emotions.

Betty felt awful, but better to hear the unpleasant news from her directly.

"Summer was pregnant with Barney's child," she finished, wincing at the cold hard truth of the words as they hung in the air.

Tears formed in Archie's eyes. He nodded to his daughter sitting on the ground in a pile of wet earth, and then wordlessly strode away, the pot-bellied pig following obediently beside him.

Betty wanted to reach out to him as she fought back tears. Instead, she stood up and brushed herself off. There was still work to do.

Murder Most Fowl

Betty and Rainbow sat in the back seat of Tom and Ben's SUV as they barreled up North Shore Road, heading to the McDonald farm. Two police cruisers and Doc Forester and two of his team members were in a black van behind them.

"So Special Agent Bruce told us that your husband is pretty whacked out," Ben Hammerton commented as he drove.

Betty met his eye after he glanced in the rearview mirror, checking to see what kind of reaction he'd get.

"Crimminy, Ben, tone it down, will you," Powder admonished his partner.

"We need to retrieve the rest of the moonshine in the barn and then see if Rainbow can convince her husband to voluntarily go for blood tests," Betty commented dryly.

"What do you think, Mrs. McDonald, do you think you can convince him to do that," Tom Powder asked gently, one arm over the seat back.

"I hope so," Rainbow squeaked.

"What was the name of the live play game he wanted to start up," Hammerton asked curiously.

"*Murder Most Fowl*," Rainbow murmured.

"So, people would come out to the farm and get the chance to kill off their enemies," Hammerton continued.

"Something like that," Betty jumped in protectively, not wanting Rainbow to say anything that she might regret. "He built a guillotine and a witch's burn pyre out behind the barn."

"Not to mention the hangman's noose in the old oak tree," Rainbow sniffed.

Betty gave Rainbow's hand a reassuring squeeze and smiled at her. The young woman smiled sadly back.

"Actually, that would be pretty cool, so long as you don't murder anybody," the junior inspector said. "You could set it up like a murder theme park with animated victims, so no one actually got hurt."

"Are you kidding me," Tom rounded on him.

"I'm serious. My sister and I love to go to war game conventions and last year we took part in a Gettysburg Civil War Reenactment. Don't knock it until you try it."

"You're one sick puppy, Hammerton," Betty snapped.

"All I'm saying is, don't be so hard on your husband, Mrs. McDonald. He might be high on that Whyte guy's LSD if the moonshine he's been drinking is contaminated, but his idea would appeal to many people and probably make you a lot more money than chicken farming," Hammerton shrugged.

"Ya think," Rainbow spat back. "His motto is *'if you can kill a chicken, you can kill anything'*."

"I love it," Hammerton laughed.

Betty and Tom exchanged a look.

"Are you sure *you* aren't high, partner," Tom cajoled him.

Hammerton grinned.

"We're here," the young inspector said, slamming on the breaks as a bevy of pheasants ran out in front of the SUV.

"Thank Heavens for small mercies," Tom muttered.

The SUV steered around the birds and finished the drive up to the house. Hammerton pulled up in front of the barn, the police cruisers and forensic van angling in beside him.

Tom opened the rear door of the SUV for Betty as his partner held open the other door for Rainbow. The two women stood looking at the open door to the barn with trepidation.

Betty's stomach twisted into knots as she thought about what they might find. She worried that Rainbow might collapse, but the young pet psychic surprised her.

"The crates of moonshine are in the chick hatchery right inside the barn door to the right," Rainbow pointed as she squared her shoulders and walked up to the barn door, her long denim skirt swishing around her ankles. She pulled her dreadlocks back into a bun and tied them up with a piece of ribbon as she walked ahead of Betty. "Please remove them quickly. I don't ever want to see another bottle of booze on my farm again."

"Yes, ma'am, but how about you let us go in first just in case your husband isn't well," Powder suggested.

"No, he's my husband," Rainbow exclaimed.

Betty wanted to high-five Rainbow. Maybe some of Vi's spunkiness had worn off on her in the past couple of days. Either way, she was proud of her new friend's tenacity.

Several grouse flew out of the barn as Rainbow entered the doorway, the police team fanning out behind her. Pigeons cooed in the rafters. Everyone ducked as white missiles splattered the ground and walls all around them.

"He's not here," she called, poking her head inside the open door to the hatchery, "but the moonshine is."

Tom signaled Forester and his team to come forward and retrieve the cartons of alcohol.

Hammerton whistled when he saw all the crates inside the hatchery.

"Is that heavy equipment that I hear," Tom asked, drawing his weapon and moving cautiously down the barn's main aisle, Hammerton following suit to his left.

"Sounds like it to me," his partner agreed.

Betty cautioned Rainbow to stay back as the two detectives crept forward, securing the area, while the forensics team and other police officers loaded the moonshine into the van.

Betty wished that Tom had allowed her to bring the shepherd, but he had been adamant about leaving the dog behind.

Tom and Ben stood at the end of the barn, hiding as best they could while they peeked around the back door.

The guillotine was finished. It stood in the middle of the meadow, its razor-sharp blade gleaming. The blade glistened, fixed as it was to the top of the guillotine mounting bracket, ready to descend with deadly force. Wood was piled high around the witch's stake and burn pyre. Frank had even built a Medieval set of stocks.

Frank had been a busy beaver.

Along the far fence, there was a holding pond. It was usually used for irrigation, but Frank had other ideas. He was using the tractor to winch a log onto a pivot. At the end of the log was a small platform, just big enough for someone to sit on. The platform hung out over the water, the perfect mechanism to act as a dunking pole.

"Betty, Mrs. McDonald, come forward," Tom ordered the two women.

Rainbow walked beside Betty, head up, eyes forward, down the barn's aisle. She stopped beside Powder.

"Is that a dunking arm," Rainbow gasped, looking out to where her husband was struggling to get the log into place

"Looks like it," Betty concluded, walking up beside her.

"Cool," Hammerton quipped.

"You're a jerk," Betty growled.

"I'm putting a stop to this," Rainbow yelled, bolting out of the barn.

"Mrs. McDonald, stop," Powder screamed.

Rainbow ignored him.

Betty raced after her.

"Betty, for Pete's sake, not you too," Powder shouted.

Tom and his partner lowered their guns as they scuttled after the women.

"Frank McDonald, what on earth do you think you're doing," Rainbow yelled, marching across the meadow.

Frank turned off the tractor and stepped down.

"Isn't it great, honey, I'm almost done? Once I mount the witch's dunk log, we can start building a website and booking want-a-be Ted Bundy's for a game of *Murder Most Fowl*," he beamed. "I added the witch stuff so we can do a medieval theme on alternate days or weekends."

"This is not happening. You take these monstrosities down," the angry woman screamed.

Betty and the two inspectors came to a halt a few feet from

them. Betty was concerned for Rainbow's safety, but Rainbow had found her voice and wasn't holding back.

"But why," her bewildered husband asked.

"Our dream was to go organic, at least mine was," she argued. "We planned on selling top end fowl. It did not include having people lopping the heads off chickens or coming here for murder weekends. You think folks will actually pay to kill a chicken just to find out what it is like to murder an innocent living thing?"

"Yeah, something like that," Frank sulked.

Frank McDonald didn't appear to be violent. Tom and Ben put away their side arms.

"You know I'm vegan and you know my family history. I've always had a hard time with the concept of raising meat birds. From the beginning, I planned on helping islanders understand their pet's problems and maybe, given all the equipment left to us, and all the fields full of herbs, even restart the herb and tea farm," Rainbow cried.

"But Rainbow, we could pay off the mortgage in no time at all with this," Frank wheedled, opening his arms to show all the torture devices that he had constructed in the past few days.

"You have to admit, he did a great job," Ken whispered to Tom.

"Now is not the time to open your big mouth," Tom told his partner.

Betty had heard enough. It was time to intervene.

"Frank, we've met before," Betty interrupted Rainbow as Rainbow was about to chastise her husband once again. "I'm Betty Bruce."

"Oh, yeah, you're the cop with the pig and cow," he said.

"That's right, I am," Betty agreed, giving Hammerton an evil look. If he said one word, Betty would have Frank show her how well the guillotine worked.

"My wife really helped your cow out," the would-be live game player said proudly.

"Yes, Peaches is doing wonderful thanks to Rainbow, but that's not the reason we're here. You see, Frank, you've been drinking a lot of moonshine lately," Betty replied calmly.

"Yeah, I know," he said, looking as contrite as a little boy who just threw a ball through a plate-glass window.

"What you didn't know is that the moonshine has been laced with LSD."

"Listen to Betty, Frank," Rainbow pleaded. "All this... it isn't you."

"I don't do drugs," Frank responded, indignant.

Rainbow ran to her disheveled sweat soaked husband. She wrapped her arms around his waist and looked up into his red-rimmed eyes.

"You've been hallucinating, babe," Rainbow crooned.

"I don't feel stoned," he mumbled. His brows knit together, and his arms hung at his sides.

"If the levels of LSD in the moonshine you've been drinking are anywhere near the one sample we tested in the lab, you're lucky to be alive," Tom Powder said, stepping forward.

"Babe, these wonderful folks want to take you to the hospital for some blood tests just to make sure that you're okay," Rainbow whispered soothingly.

Once again, Betty's admiration for the pet psychic grew.

"Okay, honey, if you say so, but I still think my witch dunker is the boss. Can't I finish it first," he asked.

Betty stifled a laugh. She had to give it to Frank McDonald. He was determined.

"By the way, have any of you seen my dog. His name is Blue. He's a Blue Heeler about yay-high," Frank asked, motioning knee high with one hand.

"Blue's been sleeping over at my place and keeping my cow company," Betty answered him.

Rainbow shot her a grateful look.

"Ahhh, that's really sweet," Frank gushed.

Tom and Ken started chuckling, unable to help themselves.

"Come on, pardner," Tom drawled, motioning Frank forward, "let's go see the doc."

"Can't we at least see if the guillotine works," Ken queried, his eyes glazing over.

Betty sighed in defeat.

Ugh!

"Oh, heck, yeah," Frank beamed. "It took me all night to get that blade to fit, not to mention cutting the sheet metal and sharpening the blade razor thin like I did."

"Really, I'd love to hear more about it," Hammerton blurted out, much to everyone's consternation. "That guillotine is radical. I've got to get a selfie with it. My sister's not going to believe it."

Rainbow stood with her hands on her hips, fury oozing out of every pour.

"Men," Betty exclaimed, knowing exactly how Rainbow was feeling.

"Hey, don't lump me into that category," Tom hissed. "Those two do not define my species."

Betty started laughing. After a moment, Rainbow did too as they followed along after Ben and Frank, who were deep in animated conversation about the torture tactics used during the Spanish Inquisition.

The Landing

The Bristling Boar was hopping as word spread about the bust at Barney's house, the confiscation of all his moonshine, Camille's arrest for the murder of Summer Rivers, and Frank McDonald's building of a working guillotine.

Betty didn't know how the news travelled so far so fast, yet at least fifty percent of Seal Island's residents were crammed into the bustling pub, many peering out of the windows at the convoy of police vehicles waiting to load onto the barge.

She supposed that during the hour wait for the tide to turn, one or more of the officers had let the news slip. She couldn't blame the officers. This was a huge bust.

Camille, hair askew and sour faced, sat handcuffed in the back seat of one of the police cruisers.

Frank McDonald sat in the back of Tom and Ben's SUV chatting animatedly with Doc Forester as the coroner monitored Frank's vital signs. Forester had taken Frank's blood samples himself and had personally made it his mission to see that Frank returned safely to his wife. He had already assured Rainbow that Frank had an amazing constitution given that he wasn't dead yet and that a helicopter evacuation wasn't necessary. He had also promised her he would make sure that Frank was delivered back to her safe and sound once Frank had a full medical check-up at the hospital.

Betty sighed with relief. The day was almost over.

One of the pub's cooks sneaked out the back door of the pub with a tray of burgers. The officers cheered when they saw him coming and eagerly descended upon him.

"Whoa, there's enough for everyone," the cook yelled above the din of the crowd in the pub as they spilled out onto the patio.

Tom and Ben jumped out of their vehicle.

"This isn't a lynch mob again, is it," Tom asked Betty.

"No, they're just making a day of it," she grinned, "but they haven't forgotten your itchy trigger finger, Ben."

The young inspector blanched, remembering how angry the mob had been when he tasered the cow instead of the pig.

"Yeah, but I'm hungry," he whined.

"I'll get you a burger," Tom told him.

"With cheese, if they have one," Ben added as he ducked back behind the wheel of the unmarked vehicle.

"When I asked you out to dinner, I wasn't quite expecting this," Powder joked as the cook handed Tom and Betty a burger.

"Thanks," Betty said to the cook. "Can you give those last three on the platter to the guys in the blue SUV?"

The cook nodded and delivered the burgers to Hammerton, Doc Forester, and Frank McDonald.

Frank took that moment to wave at all the islanders who had gathered beers in hand on the pub's deck.

They cheered and waved back.

"So how many of these folks do you think have some of Barney Whyte's tainted brew in their homes," Tom wondered aloud before taking a bite of his burger.

Betty choked on a mouthful of burger.

Tom pounded her on the back.

"Probably all of them," Betty replied sheepishly.

It was at that moment that her father and Vi strolled down the road. Gertrude, Peaches, and Champ accompanied them. The shepherd barked happily and barreled towards her.

"Champ, slow down," Betty yelled before the giant German shepherd knocked her over.

Tom chuckled and purposefully dropped a piece of his burger on the ground for the dog. Betty shot him an evil look. The dog wolfed it down.

Peaches wandered off in search of the long green shoots of grass that grew alongside the road while Gertrude made a beeline for the pub.

"Gertie," Morris Tweedsmuir yelled. "Don't you drink all the draft up on us."

A chorus of cheers erupted from the hard-drinking crowd as Gertrude bellied up to the bar.

One fisherman bent down and let Gertrude drink the rest of the beer from the bottom of his glass.

"Don't get Gertie drunk, you guys," Betty wagged a warning finger at the pub patrons. "She's in enough trouble as it is."

"I heard she dug up Barney's stash," someone yelled.

Betty shrugged her shoulders in supplication, much to the amusement of all.

"Great looking shepherd," Morris called down to her. "Tell me he isn't fixed? I'd love to breed him to my Lucy."

"He's neutered, Morris," Betty quipped with a roll of her eyes.

"He's a drug sniffer," Stew yelled as he burst out of the pub carrying a tray of draft beer.

The crowd at the pub went silent.

"Don't worry, he's semi-retired, just like Miss Bruce," Tom waved to everyone.

"And Gertrude beat him to the punch today."

Nervous laughter rippled through the men and the smattering of women leaning over the railing.

"As you've all already heard, Barney has been lacing his moonshine with LSD and God knows what," Betty yelled. "One jar we tested had lethal levels of drugs in it. If any of you have any bottles at home, either dump it out or bring it to me and leave it on my front porch and I'll make sure it gets over to the mainland to Inspector Powder."

"Is it true Camille murdered Summer?" a tall hobby farmer queried.

An angry murmur went through the crowd. A few people hissed and booed.

Betty recognized the farmer as a friend of the Rivers family. It didn't bode well for keeping order amongst the sullen mob.

Archie and Vi walked over to Betty. Archie looked like he had aged ten years since that morning. Betty was glad that he had stopped to talk to Vi. She idly wondered what was in the canvas bag slung over his shoulder.

Vi smiled sadly. She put a hand on Betty's shoulder and gave it a light squeeze.

"That's an active investigation. We have no comments at this time," Tom hollered over the hubbub that the question stirred up.

"What about Tiffany and Eliza," someone else screamed.

"Yeah, did she murder them too," yet another man called out.

There was a ripple of "yeah, we want to know" and "did she do it" along with many other questions all being asked at once.

"We couldn't answer those questions even if we knew the answers," Betty replied, trying to calm everyone down.

Betty noticed that Stew looked nervously from one to the other of the people he thought of as friends. Was that guilt or fear she saw in his face? Betty wasn't sure.

"You need to toss them something to settle their nerves, Angel," her father whispered in her ear.

"Yeah, but what," she whispered back.

Archie pulled the canvas bag off his shoulder and handed it to Betty. He and Vi exchanged a look that told Betty that they had something planned.

"I want you all to see that I'm handing Betty all the moonshine that both me and Vi had in our houses," Archie boldly stated. "And Stew, I know that you have some stashed behind the bar. Bring it out and hand it over."

Stew stammered as everyone at the landing swiveled to stare at him.

"It's okay, Stew, we won't lay any charges or notify the Liquor Control Board. Right, Inspector Powder," Betty said to Tom.

"Special Agent Bruce is correct. No questions will be asked or charges filed unless you force me to come back with another warrant," Powder said. "I'll even turn a blind eye to that dastardly pig."

Tom fixed the pub owner and the unruly bunch of islanders an award-winning smile.

The tension went out of the air.

"All right, send some men in. I think I have a crate or two in the back. It was only for personal consumption, just so you know," Stew whined.

Stew's wife burst through the open door to the pub after hearing her husband's words.

"Are you crazy, people will pay good money for Barney's Brew and now there won't be any more," she ranted, slapping her husband on the arm.

"Gwen, for Pete's sake, Stew's only doing his civic duty," a startled Morris gasped.

"You mind your own business, Morris Tweedsmuir," she growled at the red faced, red haired Scotsman.

"That's enough, Gwen," Archie barked, striding up the steps to the patio. "One woman and one man that we know of have already died because of that damnable brew. I won't tolerate any of your nonsense today. Summer was like a second daughter to me, and Barney was my best friend. My own daughter lost the love of her life and it was probably because of that moonshine too. We may never know, but you will not make a profit off it. Do you hear me?"

"Champ, stay," Betty commanded the shepherd. He sat down and obediently waited for her as she dropped the satchel of moonshine to the ground, the jars clinking together loudly. She then dashed up the steps to stand by her father's side.

Vi cried, her slim shoulders shaking with the grief of it all. She may never know if Barney or Camille Whyte or Betty's beau, Andy McDowell, were the ones who killed her sister-in-law, Eliza, or even if Eliza's death truly was a bizarre accident.

"Archie's right, Gwen, I don't want to hear another word about it either," Stew growled.

Stew threw his arms around Archie and enveloped him in a great enormous bear hug. Archie patted Stew lightly on the back, barely able to move his arms until the barrel-chested pub owner released him.

"Inspector have your officers come inside. I want that stuff gone," Stew motioned to the cops leaning against their cruisers, finishing the burgers the pub owner's cook had so graciously provided.

The pub patrons cheered as four of the officers came forward and followed Stew into the pub, his chastised wife following wordlessly at his heels.

"Gwen's not finished with him yet," Archie grimaced as he stepped down from the patio and drew the quaking old judge into his arms.

Vi wiped away her tears and hugged Archie.

"I'm going inside to make sure everything is okay," Betty advised Tom.

"Want me to come with you," Tom asked.

"I'd appreciate it if you'd hold Champ," Betty nodded towards the shepherd whose nose was quivering and hair was bristling uncomfortable from the boisterous crowd inside and outside of the pub.

"Yeah, good idea," Powder agreed, kneeling beside the restless dog.

"Dad, can you retrieve Gertrude," she queried to her father.

Archie and Vi started giggling as they glanced towards the pot-bellied pig standing between two dozen beer guzzling farmers, fishermen, and silver-haired retirees, looking pleadingly up at all the patrons, hoping that someone would give her some more beer.

Betty marched behind the officers into the pub. People reached out and patted her on the back as she did so. Betty, Gertrude, Peaches, and Champ were now the stuff of legend on Seal Island.

"It's back here in the storage room," Stew said, leading the way.

Betty and four uniformed officers followed Stew through the pub, behind the bar and into the kitchen. The deep fryer was sizzling. The air smelled like raw fish, fat, and bacon grease. Two cooks were scrambling to keep up with the orders for burgers and fish and chips.

Gwen joined in the melee.

Stew opened the door to the dry goods storage room and moved a fifty-pound bag of potatoes to one side. He pointed at the two crates of moonshine stacked between five other fifty-pound bags of potatoes.

Betty had to hand it to the pub owner. The food inspector or the

Liquor Control Board inspectors wouldn't have found those crates unless someone had told them exactly where they were.

Betty heard an angry grunt and turned to see a wild-eyed Gwen Mann standing with her hands on her hips, shear fury on her face. The vehemence that Betty saw in Gwen's expression and posture was startling in its ferocity.

"This is your fault," Gwen snarled at Betty before spinning around and stalking out of the kitchen.

Two of the police officers carried out the crates of moonshine. The other two led the way as they walked back through the kitchen, around the bar, and out of the pub.

"I had no idea he was spiking his brew, Betty," Stew told her.

Stew's face was flushed.

"I believe you," Betty replied earnestly.

Betty watched the big man crumble. With a start, she realized that this whole sordid mess must be just as hard on him as her father. Barney and Camille were his friends, too.

"You know, I'm like your dad, I like my beer. I've had a shot or two of moonshine on poker nights and a few times after hours in the pub, but not on a regular basis. It all makes sense now. There have been times when I walked home from your dad's house or stumbled up the stairs to our rooms above the pub where my legs were wobbling, and the walls were doing this psychedelic weird stuff. Once when I was walking home, the man in the moon started talking to me. I put it down to being over tired, but now I know that wasn't it at all," Stew moaned. "But Camille killing Summer? That is too much. I just can't absorb it all."

"Yes, it has hit us all hard," Betty consoled him.

Stew nodded helplessly as they made their way out to the front of the pub.

"Are you going to be okay, Stew," Betty asked, eyeing Gwen as she polished a glass behind the bar like she was going to crush it.

"Yeah, I will be," the pub owner sighed. "I'll just focus on slinging beer."

"What about Gwen," Betty asked. "She doesn't look very pleased with you."

Stew glanced over at his wife. She glared back at him.

"She's just pissed," he muttered. "Ever since she found out about Tif and me, she's been angry. It's my fault. I made the mistake of blurting out that I was in love with Tif after someone told her they had seen me leaving Tif's place one morning when I was supposed to be in the city."

"Why didn't you tell me that, Stew," Betty groaned, feeling the world fall away beneath her feet.

"I was afraid to," he admitted.

"Why?"

"Because Tiffany died less than a week later," Stew confessed.

"Oh, Stew," Betty cried out. "You should have told me."

"Well, I guess I am now," Stew admitted, slumping in defeat.

Gwen advanced upon them. She marched towards them like a Major General about to chew out the troops.

"We're busy, time to get back to work," Gwen ordered her husband.

"My wife's right. I have to go," Stew muttered, straightening his shoulders.

"We'll talk again another time, Stew," Betty whispered as he walked by her. Stew nodded sadly.

"I am sorry that I snapped at you," Gwen told Betty. "I can't believe it all. It hurts my heart."

Betty had a hard time believing anything that Gwen said, but everyone handled stress differently.

"You don't have to explain," Betty lied, not wanting Gwen to suspect the details of what Stew and she had just talked about. She had other things to worry about right now.

"It was bad manners," she answered stiffly.

"Think nothing of it. It's a shock to us all."

"You come back later with your father and have dinner with my husband and me," the little Malaysian woman added. "It's on the house; dinner between friends."

"Thanks, but I have to go to the mainland to fill out some paperwork."

Gwenn grunted and returned to serving beer as the crowd

surged inside, their mugs and glasses empty.

Betty watched the husband and wife teamwork side-by-side for a moment. The distance between them was as wide as the Gulf of Mexico, even though they stood just a few feet apart. Yes, she would definitely be questioning Stew and Gwen Mann a little more.

Betty left the pub.

Her father and Vi hadn't waited. She saw them leading Gertrude and Peaches away, back up North Shore Road, towards home.

Her shepherd sat patiently waiting for her, his eyes watching her every move, Tom Powder at his side.

"Going to bring the dog with you back to the mainland," Powder asked her, regarding her in much the same way as the dog did. "He's welcome to stay at my place, and so are you."

At that moment, the barge lowered its ramp and the police cruisers pulled forward.

The Persephone, Reggie Phoenix's trawler, had just docked, and two deckhands were securing its mooring lines.

The tall fishermen stopped to chat with the deck hands, and then Betty saw him straighten up, turn to glance at the moving police cruisers, his eyes searching the loading vehicles and the on-lookers. They settled on Betty and he strode purposefully towards her, the dock rocking gently back and forth as the big man zeroed in on her. His strides were so long that he travelled the distance in record time.

Tom turned to see where Betty was looking.

"Is that the pot farmer," he asked caustically.

"He's not a pot farmer, he's a scientist," Betty quipped, finding herself defending the grizzled fisherman. "He partnered up with Grasshopper Corporation and is developing cutting edge strains of cannabis for specialized medical conditions. Reg's got an amazing laboratory and some wonderful assistants."

"I see," Tom muttered.

"Bets, what's this I hears," Reggie asked, forcing one of the forensic vans to stop so he could reach Betty before she boarded the barge with the other officers.

Champ wagged his tail and greeted Reggie with exuberance, jumping up and licking him under the chin. Reggie laughed and hugged the shepherd.

"Down," Reggie ordered the dog.

The dog sat and yawned, its tail wagging furiously.

"It's true," Betty agreed, watching the police vehicle with Camilla in the back lurch forward. "Cam confessed to killing Summer and Barney has been lacing his moonshine with LSD."

Reggie removed his wool toque and ran his gnarled hands threw his grey curly locks. His blue eyes danced with an angry fire.

"Summer didn't deserve that and neither did that we babe she was carrying," he grimaced.

"It's interesting that the dog doesn't react to you," Tom noticed, staring down at the dog. "Are you sure he's a drug dog, Betty?"

"Who the heck are ya and what in the tar nation makes ya ask me that," Reggie growled.

Betty blanched.

What was going on here?

"Reg, this is Inspector Tom Powder. He's in charge of the investigation," Betty replied, trying to calm the situation down.

Reggie harrumphed, his glacial blue eyes narrowing.

Powder tensed, his dark brown eyes meeting the old fisherman's.

The dog growled, not knowing what to do as it looked from one man to the other.

"I have to go the mainland and file a report," Betty added. "Can you take Champ up to Rainbow's, Reggie? Frank's in the van with my friend, Doc Forester. We're taking him to get checked out at the hospital and Rainbow's all alone at the farm. I'd feel better if someone were there with her for a while and with Champ for protection."

"You think someone might be after her," Reggie gasped.

"No, but I think there are a lot of people who will want to get a good look at Frank's Madam Guillotine and the other stuff he built up there. I'd feel a lot better if you would go stay with Rainbow until I'm back. I don't want to ask my dad. He's taking all this pretty hard."

"Sure thing, Bets. Ya don't have ta worry about Rainbow or yer pup, does she, Champ," Reggie said to the dog.

The dog yawned and licked Reggie's hand.

Tom relaxed and backed off.

"Thanks. I'll be back tomorrow," she added, relieved.

"Ya just call if ya want to check in or need anything," Reggie replied, pulling her in for an embrace.

Betty blushed and sighed softly, the stress draining out of her as she inhaled the scents of lemon oil, salt water, man musk, and Polo aftershave that permeated Reggie's sweater.

"And I mean anything," was the gruff whisper in her ear. "I'll come get ya in *The Persephone* if ya need me ta."

"That's a wonderful offer, but I want to pay a visit to Barney at the hospital if the doctor says he can talk to me," she mumbled into his ear.

Reggie released her and she all but staggered backwards.

Tom grimaced.

"You okay," Tom and Reggie said in unison.

"I'm fine," she quipped, righting herself.

A horn beeped. Ben leaned out the window and whistled at them.

"It's time to go," Tom advised her.

"Champ go with Reggie," she said to the dog.

Tom handed Reggie the dog's leash.

"Come on, buddy, let's go see how Rainbow's doing," he told the shepherd, and then to Betty, "call me later so I knows yer okay."

"I will," she agreed as she raced Tom Powder to the SUV.

"What was all that about," Tom asked breathlessly as he opened the back door for her to squeeze in beside Frank and Doc Forester.

"He's a good friend," Betty said, ducking her head as she got into the vehicle.

"Looks like he's more than that," Betty heard Tom mutter as he closed the door.

Good grief, like she didn't have enough to deal with.

Betty pulled out her cell phone and texted her father, letting him know that she would be back tomorrow, and Reggie would look after Rainbow and Champ.

The SUV pulled in behind the last of the police cars.

She stared at the back of Tom Powder's head as the SUV mounted the ramp onto the barge and wondered if staying overnight with Tom Powder was a bright idea. She had mixed feelings about getting involved with the newly separated handsome inspector, even though the thought of it made her knees go weak.

And then there was good old dependable Reggie Phoenix. The grizzled fisherman was always there for her when she was in crisis mode, both as a friend and a confidant, ever ready to rescue her in the middle of the night, with or without his boat.

She doubted she would have solved the severed feet in sneakers case without his help.

And then there was the case of The Painted Lady. He had delicately watched over the young woman's body when it had washed up on shore and had refused to leave her side, afraid that no one would care like he did.

Reggie had also rescued Frank and Rainbow's chicks at a moment's notice? Without question or complaint, he had gone to stay with Rainbow and would guard her until either Betty or Frank returned home.

The other thing in his favor was Champ. The dog loved him, despite the ever-present odor of pot that permeated his skin. Occupational habit, she guessed,

Would Tom Powder do that? Would he be there for her? Would he risk his like for her friends? Would life on Seal Island suit him?

Betty didn't know Tom well enough to answer those questions.

Both men were sweet on her. The question was: was she sweet on Tom Powder or was it just lust? She knew she was sweet on Reggie in a strange, comfortable old sweater and slippers kind of way, but could it turn to more?

As the SUV thumped over the metal deck of the barge, Betty leaned back, lost in thought, until Frank McDonald burst into song.

Confessions that Aren't Confessions

Betty and Tom Powder stopped at the nurse's station. Tom flashed his badge to the harried nurse. She smiled at the charismatic inspector and said that she would check with the doctor to see if he would allow them to speak with Barney Whyte.

Nurses and attendants hustled back and forth, up and down the hall. It was just past dinner time and trays were being removed and medication disbursed to patients.

Doctors were doing their rounds.

One day had turned into two as Betty and Tom had waited patiently for Barney to recover enough that they could question him. Betty had stayed in a hotel instead of at Tom's place, much to his disappointment. It was a hard decision, but she was glad she did it.

"The doctor is in with Mr. Whyte now so you can go in. Mr. Whyte is in Room 206. It's the private room at the end of the hall on the left," the nurse advised them.

Tom and Betty sauntered down the hall, trying to stay out of the way of the hospital staff.

The doctor was just leaving Barney's room when they arrived at the door.

"Inspectors," the doctor said good-naturedly.

"Inspector, actually, just one," Tom corrected him. "This is Betty Bruce, she works as a special consultant to the RCMP, and she is a friend of Mr. Whyte's."

"How is he doing," Betty asked, her feelings mixed. On the one hand, she had known Barney for years and he had been close to her father until this happened, and on the other, he was knowingly adding drugs to the moonshine he made.

"He's stable. The surgery was textbook, and it went well, but he

95

could easily have a heart attack or a stroke if you press him too hard," the doctor cautioned them.

"We'll try not to do that, doctor, but an officer will arrive later," Tom added. "I'll be arresting him and reading him his Miranda rights if you feel he can understand them. There will be an officer outside of his door until you tell us he is fit enough to stand trial; at which time he will be remanded into our custody."

"Fair enough," the doctor agreed. "I have rounds to make. Keep it short, only a few minutes. Yes, I believe he can quite understand his rights."

Without further words, the doctor strode down the hall and disappeared into room 203.

"Well, this is it," Powder said, turning to Betty. "Are you ready, Miss Bruce?"

"As ready as ever," Betty sighed.

Tom led the way, Betty treading softly behind him.

The room smelled of disinfectant. Monitors beeped.

The shrunken man lying in the bed was a shade of his former self until he turned to look past the inspector to the neatly dressed woman in a grey blazer, grey slacks, and forest green turtle-neck sweater.

Betty felt the sharp gaze of the moonshine guru fall upon her.

"Betty," he croaked, "good of you to visit me."

"Hello, Barney," she replied, stepping around the inspector. "How are you feeling?"

"My chest feels like I've been run over by the Budweiser Clydes-dales, but other than that, I suppose I'm as good as expected. And who is this you brought with you?"

"Inspector Powder," Tom introduced himself.

"Inspector is it," Barney glowered. "I take it you got past my wife and my lawyers and have robbed me of my still then?"

"The still is being dismantled as we speak," Tom nodded in agreement.

"And we found the LSD, Barney," Betty mumbled, not as happy as she thought she'd be about confronting him.

"I see," Barney muttered, closing his eyes for a moment.

"Can I get you some water, Barney," Betty asked.

"Please," he sputtered.

Betty gave him a glass of water. He sipped the cold water from the glass, threw a straw.

"Are you here to arrest me," he asked, handing the glass back to Betty.

"Yes, sir, you're being charged with the illegal manufacturing and sales of alcohol, possession of an illegal substance, and...," Tom paused.

"And?"

"Possibly accessory to murder or attempted murder," Powder finished.

Barney sighed heavily. He looked up at the ceiling as he listened to Tom read him his rights from a card Tom had removed from his pocket.

"For the record and in front of Inspector Powder, did you know Summer was pregnant with your child," Betty asked him once Powder was finished.

"I did," Barney admitted.

"Why was Summer afraid of you, Barney," Betty demanded.

Barney was silent.

"Your wife admitted to killing Summer River," Tom added. "She's been charged with first degree murder. We are revisiting the other deaths on the island, including that of Andrew McDowell. If we find that your moonshine contributed to his death, we will add charges to the list. At this time, I would like to ask you again if you want an attorney present."

"I'd like to talk to Betty alone, inspector," Barney said to Tom Powder.

"That's up to her," Powder said stiffly.

"It's okay, Tom," she replied gently.

"Whatever he says to you won't be admissible in court," he whispered.

"I know, but I need some answers," she begged him.

"I'll be right outside the door," he conceded.

Betty waited for Tom to leave and then she rounded on the man lying immobile in the hospital bed in front of her, monitors and IV's hooked up to his chest and arms.

"Did you know what your moonshine was doing to people? To Andy," Betty blurted out.

"Of course, I did," he confessed, his eyes gleaming.

"What about Camille? Did you know that she set up Summer, so she'd fall to her death," she asked, her jaw tight and her heart pounding?

"No, but I suspected it after I heard how she died," he sighed.

"How's that?"

"Camille worked for an electrical company when I first met her," Barney acknowledged. "She had just started her apprenticeship program. She was this pretty little blond thing in work jeans and steel-toed boots with a chip on her shoulder as big as a crocodile's bite. That's what I loved about her; she wasn't afraid of hard work and knew what she wanted in life."

So, Camille had the knowledge to rig a battery to the lightning rod so when Summer grabbed it, she would make a complete circuit. The shock would be large enough to startle her, but not enough to burn the skin. If Camille were an electrician's apprentice, she wouldn't be afraid of heights either.

Betty wondered what turned Camille from a hard-working blue-collar worker into the preening trophy wife that she was today. Was living the luxury lifestyle worth the price of two lives: Summer and her baby's?

"I didn't know Summer was pregnant until she filed the paternity suit against Andy. Given that she was hardly showing and Andy's involvement with you, I knew damn well that he wasn't the father. What happened between Summer and me was an accident," he stated, his voice taking on a bitter edge that Betty had never heard before.

"It was the tenth anniversary of Summer's fiancée's death and she was pretty down," he continued. "I went over there to console her and took some moonshine and a few happy pills with me. I popped a couple in her glass of wine when she wasn't looking. I'd only wanted to cheer her up, but one thing led to another and we ended up in bed."

"You ruffied a grieving woman," Betty fumed. "That's rape, Barney."

"Yeah, well, she didn't seem that upset by it in the morning," he hissed.

"I read her diary. She was terrified of you!"

"I never would have hurt Summer. If I'd have known how much it would freak Camille out, I'd have sold the house and moved back to the States to keep her away from Summer and the kid," he snapped. "I never got the chance."

Betty gritted her teeth.

"What about Eliza and Tiffany," Betty attacked him, not caring that the doctor had warned her about raising his stress levels. "Did you or Camille have anything to do with their deaths?"

"Heck, no," he laughed. "I don't know what happened to Tiffany, but I think Andy killed her like he confessed to. He had plenty of motive to spike her chocolates with peanuts, given her involvement with your ex-husband and her dealings with him. I'm pretty sure that Eliza's death was accidental though, however bizarre it was. I mean drowning someone in their fish tank, that's Tony Soprano stuff?"

"Pretty sure?"

"I was some angry at Andy when he got involved with that paternity suit. I knew darned well that it was his idea, so I double spiked his moonshine. I knew he liked a moonshine nightcap and stopped by a few nights in a row when you weren't here and filled him full of 'bullshite' as Reggie likes to call it. I convinced him that Tiffany was blabbing about them being writing partners and her being the test subject for his sex scenes in his novels. He went off the deep end, especially when I told him about how your ex abused you. That really did it."

Barney laughed.

Betty blanched. She would have to talk with her father about discussing her private life with his buddies over poker; although, she had a feeling that from now on his poker nights would be a thing of the past.

"Go on," she encouraged him. Her stomach felt like she was going to heave, but she soldiered on.

"It's all your fault, you know. You just couldn't leave it alone. When you started getting too close for comfort and wouldn't give up looking into the lady's deaths, I worked on Andy until I had him convinced, he was a killer. I slipped him quite the cocktail before he marched over to Vi's that day, all revved up and bent on murder. When that wonderful pig of yours pushed him over the cliff, it was a perfect crime."

"So when my father and I caught you coming out of Andy's house, you had just removed the jar of moonshine from the liquor cabinet, hadn't you," she asked him, suddenly realizing why there had been no moonshine in the cupboard. Betty was relieved. She hadn't lost her mind after all.

"Yep," Barney laughed.

Betty slumped forward, defeated.

Was she really the catalyst for four deaths? How was she going to prove any of this?

"I'm kind of tired," Barney croaked. "I'd like you to leave now."

Betty turned away and headed for the door, but before she left, she had to ask one more question.

"Why did you spike the moonshine, Barney," she asked, her voice echoing off the walls of the small room.

"For fun," Barney grinned, and then nodded off to sleep.

Betty's head was reeling as she left room 206. She felt powerless against the guilt that threatened to overwhelm her. Had Eliza's death truly been accidental? Had that triggered a calamity of events that resulted in Tiffany's and Andy's deaths? If she hadn't gotten involved with Andy in the first place, would Summer and Andy have to come to her for help? The same questions went around and around in her head.

"Are you okay," Tom asked her with concern. "You're white as a sheet."

"I'm fine, but I want to go home," Betty whimpered. She hated how weak she sounded, but she couldn't help herself.

"I can take you to the ferry to Vancouver Island, but you won't be able to catch the passenger ferry until tomorrow afternoon. What did he say in there that's shaken you up so badly?"

"He set Andy up," she croaked, "but I can't prove it."

"Why is that?"

"The only one who can prove it is Andy, and he's dead."

"Oh," Tom answered helplessly. "Why don't you come and stay at my place tonight. I'll make sure you get to the early morning ferry to Vancouver Island. No strings attached."

"Thanks, but I'd appreciate it if you'd take me to the hotel so I can check out and then drop me off at Horseshoe Bay."

"Are you sure," Tom asked worriedly.

"I'm sure," she said, offering him a weak smile.

She had a lot to think about, possibly things she needed to atone for.

In that moment, she knew with all her heart where she belonged, and who she needed to call to take her there.

Old Spice & Goddesses

Betty stood on the pier at Horseshoe Bay as the sun set over the Strait in a brilliant display of red and pink above the dark grey water and the shadows of the night. Stars twinkled overhead.

She had changed into blue jeans and her favorite red and black lumberjack shirt. Her attire matched the colors of the sunset.

Red sky at night, sailor's delight, she thought, her mouth lifting in what anyone looking would think was a sad smile.

Now that she was retired, she had let her hair grow out. It fell loose about her shoulders, stray strands lifting in the evening breeze.

Lights were already on in the cliff top homes that looked down on the marina and ferry terminal.

Hundreds of people walked the sidewalks along the main street where restaurants and shops were full to overflowing as the tidal wave of people descended upon the area for the start of the Easter weekend.

The B.C. Ferry, The Queen of Cowichan, had just docked and a couple hundred drivers of cars and trucks were getting ready to unload.

Betty was glad that she didn't have to board the ferry for the return trip to Vancouver Island.

The running lights of *The Persephone* were now visible as the reconditioned trawler slowly eased its way around the point and into the docks.

Betty slung her backpack over her shoulder and wandered to the open berth where Reggie would be docking his boat.

Reggie's happy reply to her phone call to ask him to come pick her up at the docks echoed through her mind.

"I'd like to take you up on your offer," she almost sobbed into the phone. She was glad that she asked Tom Powder to wait for her in the lobby while she retrieved her backpack and clothes. It gave her a chance to dissolve into a short-lived bout of self-pity after her visit to the hospital.

"Bets, what's wrong," his baritone voice boomed over the speaker on her cell phone.

"I can't really talk about it right now," she said huskily. "I'm packing up and checking out of the hotel. Tom has offered to drop me off at Horseshoe Bay, but then I won't get home until tomorrow."

"Yer at a hotel," he asked gruffly.

Betty thought she heard a modicum of relief in his voice.

"Yes, but not for long," she replied, her voice cracking. Damn her emotions, she cursed herself. It wasn't like her to let herself get so affected by someone else's words and theories.

"I should be at the ferry terminal within the hour, but I'd really like to get home tonight instead of finding another hotel on the big island."

"I'm on my way," Reggie replied. "There's a berthing bay they keep open at the far end of Sewell's Marina. I'll pick ya up there."

Suddenly, she realized that she hadn't asked if it was safe to leave Rainbow alone or if there had been any trouble in the past couple of days.

"Are you still at Rainbow's? Is it okay to leave her alone," Betty whispered, not fancying running for the Queen of Cowichan at the ferry dock if Reggie thought Rainbow needed him.

"I am, but don't ya worry about it," the old fisherman assured her. "The lookie-loos got the drift real quick when me and Champ escorted 'em none too gentle like off'n the property."

Betty wiped a tear from her eye and chuckled at the thought of Reggie's bear of a form carting the likes of some of the residents of Seal Island off the McDonald farm.

"Ain't nobody showed up after the second night," he continued. "I'll give Morris a shout and ask him ta check in on our Rainbow."

"That's great. I'll see you when you get there."

Betty breathed a sigh of relief and ended the call.

The Persephone's bell chimed twice as Reggie expertly guided the trawler in, her engines chugging. Water churned out of the stern as the old wooden boat gently bumped against the dock's bumpers.

Reggie's broad shouldered and rugged form was visible inside the pilot house.

Betty threw her backpack onto the boat and leapt onto the deck before Reggie had time to lend her a hand.

"Jumping Jiminy, Bets, that was a big leap," he drawled opening the door to the cabin for her as she strolled across the deck. "Are ya part bull frog?"

"Maybe," she said, trying to sound chipper, but even to her ears, her voice sounded flat.

"Ya should have waited. I'd a put out a ladder. My heart's a' pounding on what could'a happened if ya fell between the dock and my girl, Persephone."

"Sorry, Reg, I just want to go home and didn't think," she gasped, looking at the black water between the boat and the dock. Reggie was right. If she had taken a misstep, it would have been her last.

Reggie lifted the backpack from her shoulder and escorted her into the pilothouse.

"We'll get going lickety-split so we don't have ta wait fer the Queen to get loaded," he nodded towards the ferry as the cars drove off and the ferry personnel readied the vehicles waiting at the terminal for loading.

Betty smiled grimly and sat in the seat beside the Captain's chair.

Reggie turned the wheel and pushed the throttle forward. *The Persephone* bucked and grumbled as it pulled away from the dock and out into the narrows that lead into Horseshoe Bay.

Betty remained silent, letting Reggie focus on exiting the harbor.

Reggie cast concerned glances her way.

She wasn't surprised. Betty didn't recognize the haunted eyes in the reflection that stared back at her from the boat's window. Those eyes had been a familiar sight in the mirror after Andy died and during the years she had spent married to Jim, but it had been a year or more since had she looked that haggard.

In some ways, her marriage, as bad as it was, had made her a better cop and a much better detective. She was a good deal more compassionate and a lot stronger in her resolve and strength of character because of it.

She turned her attention to the startlingly beautiful night. On the western horizon, the sun had disappeared, leaving faint traces of a rainbow of color. Fairy lights glowed inside cottages, sparks of humanity on a peaceful stretch of coastline, some lights dancing like fireflies on the water as the boat cruised by.

Above, the sky was alive with stars. The North Star burned brightly, and Betty could see both the Big and Little Dipper.

The light roll of the ship and the soft chatter of water rolling off its keel worked at silencing the endless series of questions that rattled around in her mind like a merry-go-round. Guilt was consuming her. She hadn't eaten since lunch.

"So are ya going ta tell me what's eating ya up," Reggie asked gently.

Betty turned to look at him. Her heart swelled at the concern she saw in his deep blue eyes. The dash lights illuminated his face with soft white, creating a halo around his scruff of grey hair and whiskered chin.

Betty sighed wearily.

"Barney confessed to drugging Andy. Andy believed all the lies Barney told him about Eliza, Tiffany and Summer. Somehow, he convinced Andy that he had killed them because they were out to ruin his reputation and destroy his relationship with me," Betty trembled.

She stopped. It was hard to breathe. She took a deep breath and let it out slowly, fighting the anxiety that even talking about it brought on.

"Barney waited until I was in Vancouver or at dad's place to get the ball rolling. Vi was on the case with me and when she confronted Andy on the pier that day, he must have believed everything that Barney had told him," she continued. "Andy spiraled out of control at an alarming rate after that."

"By Jesus, that's nasty, even fer him," Reggie growled. "I always knew that Barney had a dark side, but that's just plain evil."

"Evil is the word for it," Betty agreed. "And there is really no way to prove it, not in a court of law, anyway."

The two were silent as Reggie guided the trawler in the middle of the Strait of Georgia, heading north by north-west up the coastline.

Reggie pushed the throttle forward, and the trawler sped up, its bow slicing through the waves.

Betty rubbed the back of her neck. Her muscles ached.

"Ya know, we don't have ta go back to the island," Reggie said, his voice matching the rumble of the big trawler's diesel engines.

"What do you have in mind," she asked nervously.

"There's two beds downstairs," he replied with mirth. "So, don't go getting yer knickers in a twist. It just seems to me that a night on the water'd do ya good. There's a cove off'n Protection Island where we can moor and just sit on the deck and watch the moon rise over ta water. I got Bailey's fer coffee, a case of beer, and I think there's a bottle of wine in the galley. If'n ya don't want a drink, I still got some of Summer's teas too."

Betty blushed. A lump rose into her throat. Reggie's kindness was overwhelming, and she felt a bit off balance. In a way, hadn't she been thinking of this recently when she booked the hotel instead of staying with Tom Powder.

It was time to make up her mind.

"That would be nice, Reg," she replied softly, her heart feeling as light as a bird's.

Reggie's smile lit up his face.

"Good thing, I'm heading that way then," he mumbled.

Betty giggled. The giggle turned into a laugh, and the laugh into a sob.

"Ah, Bets, I'm sorry if'n I upset ya," the Old Spice guy stammered.

Reggie wore his heart on his sleeve. He loved her. She saw it in his eyes and heard it in his words. With a start, she realized that she had known he had for a long time.

Betty stood up and leaned in towards him. She rested her head on his shoulder as he wrapped one arm around her, the other still fixed to the ship's wheel.

"You didn't upset me, Reggie," she murmured. "You're my lighthouse in a storm. It's taken me a long time to realize that. I don't have many friends, and you were always there. You're probably the only man I ever trusted completely. Even when we were in high school, if any guy messed with me, there you were, my guardian angel. I missed you when you left to go work with your father."

"That's because I love ya, Bets, always have," he confessed. "Ya didn't really need me, ya never did. I know I'm not good enough fer ya. I'm not educated like Andy was and I don't have no fancy job like that Tom Powder."

"Schooling isn't everything and you are an educated man. You're educated in life. You're too good for me, Mr. Phoenix," she replied breathlessly.

Reggie turned his head to look down at her and Betty rose onto her tippy toes and kissed him lightly on the lips. He smelled of musk, lavender, thyme and rosehips.

"You smell like flowers," Betty murmured.

"I was teaching Rainbow how ta get the herbs growing again. She's gonna start up the tea farm," he replied huskily.

"That's marvelous."

Reggie grunted and pulled her into his lap and kissed her passionately.

Betty felt all her problems slip away. Her mind went blank. For the moment, she simply let go and let herself be carried away by the feel of Reggie's strong lips against hers.

After a moment, he chuckled and pulled away from her.

"We'll be settling down with King Neptune if'n I don't keep my eyes open fer dead heads in the water," he joked.

Betty laughed lightly and continued to lean against him. *The Persephone* was aptly named, the goddess of spring and Queen of the Underworld. She was a beautiful goddess, known for good harvests and fertility.

"And by the way," Reggie consoled her. "Ya have more friends than ya know on Seal Island. Whatever ya need ta do ta find out what really happened ta Eliza and Tiffany, then ya do it. They were kind people, and so are you. Don't ya ever forget that, Betty Bruce."

Betty gave him a quick kiss on the cheek and then dodged away before he could grab her.

"Where ya going," he asked alarmed.

"To put the coffee on," she quipped, opening the hatch to go down below. "It's going to be a long night."

Reggie smiled.

"Don't forget the Baileys," he suggested merrily.

"I won't," she winked at him.

Retribution

Betty sat beside Reggie in the pilothouse of the trawler sipping a coffee. She was tired, but not as heart sore as the day before. Reggie had talked her into spending another day on the water. She needed time to think and had quickly agreed. One day had turned into two as they made their way up the coast of Vancouver Island to Desolation Sound.

Even though Betty had grown up on Seal Island, she had never taken any trips outside of the immediate area until she had hired Reggie to take her to the small village of Lund in search of a cemetery by the sea and to view the place that Reggie called, the Glory Hole. The Glory Hole was a funnel carved into the cliff by the tides, where water shot through it like a giant saltwater geyser. That was the first time she had been alone with Reggie for any length of time.

She had realized then, and even more so now, how much she had missed in focusing on her career. Except for the occasional kayak trip around the island, she had never truly taken the time to explore the world around her.

It thrilled her when they had seen both killer and humpback whales during their stay in Desolation Sound, plus a myriad of seabirds and sea lions. It didn't take much arm twisting for her to agree to spend the night moored in a private cove off the coast.

Betty was immensely grateful to the scruffy bearded man piloting the trawler back to Seal Island. He was gentle and kind. His warmth and huggable nature hadn't eased the guilt that Barney had instilled in her, but it had quieted the jumble in her mind. She was embarrassed to have fallen into his arms so quickly, but he had allayed her fears with unbridled passion and selfless determination.

She had been so self-reliant all her life that letting go and opening up to a man had been difficult. It was funny that it took Rainbow's calling him the 'Old Spice guy' and her gentle smile whenever Betty mentioned Reggie's name for Betty to realize what was right in front of her all the time - a unique gem of a man with an open heart and eyes for nobody else. Betty had taken Reggie's stalwart friendship for granted for over thirty years, oblivious to his quiet signs of devotion. She didn't intend to spend the next how many years she had left in her life with blinders on.

In the past twenty-four hours, the two of them had enjoyed the simple pleasures of being on the boat away from civilization and the disorderliness of life. Now, Betty's resolve to poke deeper into Tiffany's and Eliza's deaths, despite Barney's bitter words, was returning as they got closer to the Seal Island landing.

"I don't want ta harp on it, but I want to remind ya before we dock that ya need ta push Barney out of yer mind," Reggie drawled, as if reading her thoughts.

"I know, but the guilt over the fact that I may have inadvertently caused all of this is still there," she said.

"I want ya ta listen to me 'cause I've lived on that island longer than you have even though we were both raised there," Reggie continued, his voice taking on an edge, "but men like Barney Whyte and Stew Mann are born liars. They are what ya call Masters of Deception. Tiffany was darn good at it too."

"What do you mean by that," Betty gasped.

"Men and women that cheat and lie ta get what they want aren't past turning folks' feelings inside out," Reggie continued. "I met Camille Whyte and Gwenn Mann before they got married ta Barney and Stew. They were tough cookies, but they were nice gals. It was the constant cheating of their men that turned 'em bitter and angry. All they wanted was ta get even and hurt 'em where it hurt most, which in those two fellas cases was their pocketbook."

Betty pondered his words. Money and retribution for a broken heart were excellent motivations to commit murder. Camille's actions had already proved that. What about Gwen? She had seen

Gwen's anger, but just how nasty was her nasty side?

"Why Tiffany," she asked quietly as Reggie guided the trawler in.

"Don't get me wrong, I thought the world of Tiffy. She was pretty and smart and funny, but she loved money and the making of it. She was always wheelin' and dealin'," he muttered as he spun the wheel, expertly guiding the ship between the red and green channel markers. "She couldn't say 'no' to booze or sex and didn't care who it hurt, either herself or whatever fella she bedded. I was glad when she finally got it together and joined AA, but she'd already hurt a lot of folks by then."

"Are you talking about Cam and Gwen specifically," she asked, rising to stand by his side as he finished docking.

"Them and Andy," he nodded. "Tiffy told me she put the screws ta him over the commission split on the books she co-wrote with him. She was drunk as a skunk by then, and I don't think she ever remembered telling me. I've read her stuff and a couple of his novels. Ya sure wouldn't have thought she put much effort into working with Andy 'cause they are about as alike as a Coho salmon and a Mallard duck."

Betty laughed.

Reggie smiled down at her.

The love in his eyes made her wish that they had never left Desolation Sound.

"I'll keep that in mind," she said lightly.

"Ya do that," he replied, "and ya make sure ya let me know what yer doing so's I can make sure ya got more than just Champ and Gertie fer back-up. They're good ta have around, but I got more invested in keeping ya safe than even they do."

The two kissed briefly as the dock hands looped *The Persephone's* mooring lines around the dock tie downs.

It surprised Betty to see that her father and Judge Bone waited for them at the landing. They walked up the dock towards the trawler, hand in hand.

Betty grinned. It looked like she wasn't the only one who had found romance in the past few days.

She flushed, feeling the heat rise from the tip of her toes to her ears. What would her father have to say about her obvious involvement with Reggie Phoenix? She knew it would be impossible to keep it a secret and she wasn't going to lie about their relationship to her father or anyone else.

"Just so ya know, I texted yer pa that I had whisked ya away on *The Persephone* and wouldn't return ya until ya were less stressed," he joked.

"Did you now? Cheeky, cheeky."

"I did," he grinned. "So, are ya less stressed?"

"I am," she said and planted another kiss on his lips.

Reggie pulled her close, and they kissed long and hard.

"By the saints, but ya got my blood boiling," he whispered huskily.

"Hold that thought, Popeye, I have some more sleuthing to do and I want to pick up Champ at Rainbow's," she gushed.

"I'll pick up Champ after I check on the kids to make sure they haven't forgotten ta feed the chicks while I was gone. I'm gonna get Morris ta help me take 'em back to Rainbow's farm. You go have lunch with yer pa and Vi and let me know if yer stress levels get out of control."

Betty laughed and broke away from his embrace.

Reggie shut down the engines and hustled about, securing the boat, while Betty grabbed her bag and then made her way out to the deck to greet Vi and her father.

"Hey, pops," she cried, leaping from the boat to the deck in one bound. "Good to see you, Vi."

"Bets, I told ya not ta do that," an exasperated voice bellowed behind her.

Betty grinned and waved a hand over her head without turning around.

"Ruddy woman's gonna give me grey hair," Reggie rumbled.

"Too late," she called back.

Reggie shook his head and disappeared into the cabin.

"You look happy," Vi beamed, the glint in her eye matching Betty's own.

"You two look pretty happy yourself," Betty replied with a grin.

"Am I missing something here," Archie asked.

"Apparently so," Vi quipped. She squeezed Archie's hand. He shook his head in puzzlement.

Betty laughed.

"I'm starving. We didn't eat lunch. Reggie offered to fry up some canned ham, but I wanted fresh veggies," Betty chirped.

"Ah, well, the pub it is then," her father said happily. "A burger, fries, and a pint will do me nicely. You know, Angel, I don't miss the moonshine one little bit."

"That's good, Dad. Where's Peaches and Gert," Betty asked as the three of them sauntered down the dock and across the landing to the Bristling Boar Pub.

"Oh, she's been sulky ever since you left. I figure I'd leave the two of them at Vi's happily destroying her garden for awhile," Archie replied.

"They were doing quite a good job of it when we left," Vi giggled, seemingly not too upset by the idea of the cow eating the tops off her flowers and the pig digging holes in the vegetable patch.

"Have I missed anything interesting other than you two hooking up," Betty laughed.

"How'd you know," Archie blushed.

"Guess, I'm psychic," Betty guffawed.

"It's easy to tell, dear," Vi consoled Archie.

"Well, there is one thing," Archie murmured, changing the subject.

The trio stopped at the bottom of the steps to the pub.

"What's that," Betty asked.

"That," he nodded towards the truck coming down North Shore Road.

Betty turned around in time to see Ben Hammerton driving a pickup truck pulling a flatbed trailer behind it. A woman stood beside him. She was the splitting image of the godlike detective: blond hair, angular jaw, handsome features. The woman was obviously his sister. Frank's guillotine and the giant oak stocks that Frank had made were tied down to the flatbed trailer.

"Hey, Special Agent," Ben called to her.

"What on earth," Betty exclaimed. "Hammerton, what have you got yourself into?"

"Isn't it great? Frank sold them to me," he said excitedly. "You must come to me and my sister's Halloween party. It's going to be sensational!"

"So long as you don't taser anyone, I'm good," she yelled back. "And make sure you have your badge ready for the first cop who pulls you over lugging that thing around."

The detective gave her a thumb's up while his sister waved goodbye as Ben drove down to the barge loading ramp.

"At least that's one thing I no longer have to worry about," Betty mumbled.

"Aren't you glad that you're not his neighbor," Vi quipped.

The three of them laughed and made their way into the pub.

The pub was busy given it was the Saturday of the Easter long weekend. They grabbed the first table that became empty.

Betty noticed that the same pretty bartender that Barney had been ogling was on behind the bar, working hard alongside Gwen Mann.

Stew was helping the waitresses serve food on the floor.

Gwen walked over with a tray of draft beer for the three of them as soon as they got seated.

"I'd recommend burgers all around today," Gwen announced.

"Works for me," Archie piped up.

"Can I have mine with salad, Gwen," Betty asked. "I don't care if it's Caesar or a Chef's salad."

"Me too," Vi chimed in.

Gwen pursed her lips and glared down at them.

"I can't guarantee it today," she said, whirling around.

"Does that woman ever smile," Vi whispered.

"Not for a long time," Archie muttered under his breath.

"Reggie told me she used to be really nice," Betty added conspiratorially.

"What happened," Vi asked quietly.

"I can answer that," Archie murmured. "She married my buddy.

He's a great friend, but hard on his wives."

As if sensing he was being talked about, Stew hustled over to say hello after dropping off two plates of fish and chips at the table across from them.

"And so it begins," he chirruped. "Tourist season is here."

"With a bang," Archie agreed.

"Guess we better keep the kids in line, Pop," Betty said to her father.

"Good luck with that," Stew guffawed.

Stew turned his attention to the pretty bartender who was earning her wages behind the bar. She was a blond with legs that went on forever and a smile as big as Texas. By the grins of the men seated at the bar, they were enjoying her company too.

Betty noticed Gwen watching her husband as he absently continued to stare at the new bartender. Her eyes narrowed. Her mouth set in a grim line.

"Gwen was good enough to come over and take our orders right away," Betty said to Stew.

"What's that," the startled pub owner asked, snapping his head around to look at Betty.

"If you'd stop staring at Melanie like she was the last woman on earth, you'd have heard my daughter say that Gwen's already looked after us," Archie replied, his voice taking on a hard edge.

"Just looking to see if she needs help," Stew stammered.

"Yeah, right," Archie growled.

Stew grinned and walked off. He joined his wife and Melanie, the new bartender behind the bar.

Betty watched the goings on in the pub with interest. Within a few minutes, Stew was laughing and flirting with the bartender. The more he did so, the quieter and angrier Gwen got until she disappeared into the kitchen and never came out.

"So, Angel, any news to impart," her father asked, breaking her out of her reverie.

"I saw Barney at the hospital," she replied. "The surgery went well. He wasn't surprised to hear of his wife's confession and that she was being charged with first degree murder."

Archie slumped in his chair and stared morosely into his beer. Vi squeezed his hand. He looked up, his face as grim as Stew's wife's had been.

"It's a sad thing," he said with a shake of his head.

"But life goes on, Archie," Vi consoled him.

"Aye, and I'm grateful that I have you, Vi, and such a wonderful daughter," Archie replied.

Betty had never seen her father look so vulnerable. She decided not to mention any of her other suspicions at the table.

"There is one thing that I do need to tell you, Dad," Betty said and then grinned. "It may or may not make you happy, but I'd rather you heard it from me."

"And what's that, Angel puss," he mumbled.

Vi glanced at Betty. Their eyes met. Vi nodded in approval.

"As you know by Reggie's text," Betty said, her voice warbling. "Reggie and I spent a few extra days on his boat. We were in Desolation Sound. We had a marvelous time and, well, one thing led to another."

"He didn't take advantage of you, did he," Archie growled. "I don't care how big he is or how much younger, I'll knock his block off if he did."

Betty and Vi burst out laughing.

Archie looked from one to the other of them, totally confused.

"No, Pop, he didn't take advantage of me, I took advantage of him."

A winter's snowstorm blowing in on a sunny Easter weekend couldn't have stunned her father more, Betty realized.

"It's been coming for quite some time," Vi whispered in his ear. "Reggie's been in love with your daughter for as long as I've known him."

"How did you know that?" Betty gasped.

"It was obvious to everyone but you and your father, dear," Vi said, and then grinned.

"I guess I can live with that," Archie mumbled. "He's a good man, I suppose."

"He's a very good man," Betty agreed, leaning back in her chair.

Gwen burst out of the kitchen's swinging doors, three plates in her hand. She stopped short when she saw her husband leaning in close to Melanie and whispering something in her ear.

The bartender's giggle reminded Betty of Tiffany. In fact, her looks were like Tiffany's too. She doubted that Gwen had anything to do with hiring the lovely young lady.

Gwen stormed around the bar and strode towards their table. She deposited the three plates of burgers in front of them and stalked off. Betty swore she could see the smoke coming out of her ears.

"I guess they were out of greens," Vi said innocently, noticing the lack of salad on her plate.

Betty looked down at her plate. The fries were crisp and not out of a package. She sighed. She really had wanted a salad.

"But it's hot, hot, hot," Archie sang, making like he was playing the maracas.

Vi chuckled.

Betty smiled as she thought back to what Reggie had told her about Camille and Gwen, and at what Tom Powder had told her about Gwen's jealous streak and the assault charges. Retribution can be nasty. Exactly how far would Gwen go to keep her man, she wondered, and would the innocent bartender be the next to bizarre death on Seal Island?

She bit into her burger. It was magnificent. Juice squirted out of the sides of her mouth. The smoky taste of barbeque beef and the tangy taste of dill pickle made her mouth water.

In between burger bites, a plan to expose Gwen as the murderer that Betty believed she was formed in Betty's mind. The plan depended on how much Stew wanted to get into Melanie's pants. By the lascivious look he was giving Melanie, it would not be difficult at all.

From there, she simply needed a little help from her father and her friends.

Murder by Moonlight

If everyone played their roles right, then Tiffany's killer would be revealed tonight. It was a dangerous game she was playing, and she prayed that no one would get hurt, especially the people she was setting up.

It was irresponsible, but everyone around the table had agreed that it was a necessary evil.

Betty sighed as she looked around the table from one friend to the other, her gaze finally settling on her father. His role was the key to a successful mission. She had worried it would be too much for him. He had rallied at the thought of finding out once and for all if Eliza's death really was an accident or if Andy, or someone else, had killed her. Her father had loved Eliza dearly, as a friend and as a companion after they both had lost their spouses. It was ironic that he now found consolation with Eliza's sister-in-law, Violet Bone.

Betty sat at the table with Frank and Rainbow McDonald, her father, and Vi. There was an empty chair beside her. Reggie was the last to get there.

Almost to the second she thought of him, Reggie opened the door to the pub and strode across the dining room with a jaunty step, not a care in the world. Betty almost didn't recognize him.

Reggie wore the blue turtleneck shirt that she liked so much and clean blue jeans. His curly mop of hair was neatly trimmed. He had shaved off his beard.

Who knew that her beau was so handsome under all that fur? She hadn't seen him clean shaven since his senior year in high school. That was a long time ago.

"Whoa, Reggie, looking good," Rainbow remarked.

"You clean up nice, buddy," Frank agreed.

"Close your mouth, Angel, you're catching flies," her father chortled.

Reggie rounded the table and stooped over to give Betty a kiss before sitting down.

There was a giant gasp from the dozen patrons in the pub, including Stew and Gwen who stood polishing glasses behind the bar. Melanie was just arriving for her shift. She wandered behind the bar and tugged on her black bar apron.

Stew ambled towards them with a mug of draft for Reggie, a silly grin plastered to his face.

"Well now, that's gonna set the island grapevine to buzzing," Stew said cheerily.

"I expect it will," Reggie chimed, "but ya don't need to be starting it."

"Too late for that, my friend," Stew slapped Reggie on the back. He nodded towards the tables where folks were busy texting on their phones.

"It doesn't matter," Betty said as she entwined her fingers threw Reggie's. "Everyone was bound to find out sooner or later."

Reggie chuckled.

"So. what do ya think," he asked Betty, a mischievous glint in his eyes as he placed her hand on his cheek.

"I like it," she purred.

Everyone at the table laughed.

"New love. Ain't it grand," Stew quipped before taking everyone's order.

"Looks like you got a little something new going on the side," Archie whispered to Stew as Stew leaned forward to pick up their menus.

"Shhh, don't say that too loud," Stew mumbled back. "Gwen would kill me or Mel if she heard that."

"Ahh, but you're not denying it," Archie muttered under his breath.

Stew winked at Archie before pulling away.

Gwen and Stew served up their lunches. Gwen was pleasant for once as she deposited a three-piece fish and chip dinner in front of Reggie.

"I'm glad for you," she said to Betty. "He's much better than that writer. No decent man talks bad about his mother. Too many women he had. I was glad when your pig killed him."

"Thank you, Gwen... I think," Betty replied, puzzled. Andy was popular with the ladies, but he wasn't the type to fool around as far as she knew. He didn't get along with his mother, but she couldn't remember Andy ever bad-mouthing Marilyn. Gwen's comment surprised Betty.

"And you're lucky too, big guy," Gwen said, poking Reggie on the shoulder with one finger.

And then Gwen did something that no one had seen for a long time... she smiled.

Betty's stomach flip-flopped. Maybe she was wrong about Gwen. What if she was causing trouble where there was none?

"Hey, Gwen," Rainbow queried, "we're going on an overnight trip on Reggie's boat with Betty, Archie and Vi. Do you know of anyone who could farm sit for the night?"

"Yeah, we'll feed and water the chicks before we go. They're growing fast. They need to be locked in the barn at night or the raccoons will get them," Frank added.

"The dogs are coming with us," Rainbow volunteered.

"Gert and Peaches are staying there too so we can all go without worrying about them getting into trouble. They'll be happy to just weed-eat the lower pasture," Betty conceded.

"I don't know anyone," Gwen replied.

"Maybe Morris," Stew said thoughtfully.

"No, I already asked him and he's expecting. Two of his goats are gonna deliver any day and one of 'em had trouble before," Reggie nodded, stabbing a French fry with his fork.

"Do you think maybe Melanie would stay over," Archie asked. "I know she hasn't found a permanent place to stay yet on the island and I expect the cabin's rented given its Easter weekend."

"That's a splendid idea, I'll ask her," Stew agreed, turning toward the bar.

"Hey, Mel, want to farm sit for the night for Frank and Rainbow," Stew bellowed. "You can play with their chickies."

"Sure, that would be fun," the young bartender replied.

"Awesome, thanks," Frank waved at her.

Gwen's smile quickly dissipated. She scowled as she marched back to the bar.

Betty saw her father wink at Stew. Stew grinned and winked back.

The stage was set.

Betty found she wasn't that hungry anymore as she played with her fries.

Reggie elbowed her gently.

"It's not too late ta change yer mind," he whispered in her ear. "Ya can call it all off and we'll just go boating."

"What's the worst that could happen," she mumbled back. "Nothing happens and I spend a long cold night in a barn with Tom and a pot of coffee, and then wind up with egg on my face in the morning."

"I'd still prefer ta be there with ya than that Powder fella," he argued, "and ta wipe the egg off'n yer face if ya need it."

Betty chuckled and gave him a quick peck on the cheek.

"None of that in front of your old man," Archie warned the couple. "It ain't right, I tell you."

Reggie was about to make a joke, but Archie raised his hand for him to stop.

"Don't even think of calling me Pops," he barked.

"Nope, I don't reckon I'll ever do that," Reggie admitted.

The lunch went on as planned. Before she knew it, they were done and heading off to make a very public exit on *The Persephone*.

***

Tom and Betty sat in the dark in lawn chairs in the McDonald's barn's hay loft, wrapped in blankets and drinking coffee. Tom had rigged a series of hidden cameras around the house earlier. He had also hidden a camera in the loft that pointed towards the front lane so they could see who was coming and going. Live streams of the kitchen, living room, bedroom, and front entrance flashed across the small panels on his laptop screen. The grey and black images cast shadows over their own faces.

Betty checked the time using her cell phone. It was 11:58.

"Melanie should arrive shortly. The pub closes at 11 p.m. and then she has to get the stragglers out," Betty remarked. "I'm not sure how she'll get here."

"I can't believe you talked me into this crazy scheme," Tom yawned.

Betty yawned too. It had been an eventful day.

So far everything had gone as planned. Reggie had taken *The Persephone* over to the French Creek Harbor to pick up Tom Powder after her father, Vi, Rainbow, Frank, the two dogs, and Betty, had climbed aboard. They waved like royalty embarking on a world tour as they left the marina. It was supposed to be an overnight outing to Desolation Sound.

Betty wished ruefully that they were there now, sitting on the boat's deck, drinking wine, sharing a fondue, watching the sunset and listening to whale song.

She had called Tom the night before to tell him of her wild scheme to get Gwen to confess to Tiffany's murder, and maybe even Eliza's too. He had thought she'd lost her mind. She was flabbergasted when he said he was coming and would bring some surveillance equipment along. Tom confessed he wasn't going to bring a team based on her hairbrained idea, not without proper evidence. He didn't want to even ask a Judge or the District Attorney if it was legal.

Betty bit her lip.

There were so many things that could go wrong.

Betty wished that Champ were with her but hauling the dog up the steep ladder into the hay loft was a bad idea. She also didn't want him barking at the wrong moment. The German shepherd had whined its heart out when Reggie rowed Tom and her to shore and returned to the trawler alone.

Reggie wasn't very happy with her either.

He'd get over it, she reasoned, and so would the dog.

"There she is," Tom mumbled pointing at the screen.

Betty saw the pale-faced image of the bartender arriving on a mountain bike, a backpack on her back, as she cycled up to the log cabin.

She went inside.

Rainbow and Frank had left a kitchen light on.

They saw him flick lights on in the rest of the small cabin.

"When do you think Stew might show up," Tom whispered in the dark.

"Probably not for a couple of hours. He'd want to make sure that Gwen was sound asleep first," she mumbled.

Tom sighed wearily.

Betty poured herself another cup of coffee.

They heard as well as saw Melanie leave the house and head straight towards the barn. She carried a flashlight. The beam hit the lens of the small camera on the tripod perched on the lip of the small twin doors leading into the hayloft.

"What do you think she's doing," Tom gasped, alarmed.

Betty stifled a laugh.

"She's coming to play with the chickies," she guffawed as the flashlight beam lighted up the path between the house and the barn.

The pony-tailed bartender slid the lower barn doors open and stepped inside.

They heard her searching for a light switch down below them. She found it and turned it on. The chicks in the big pen that used to belong to the pheasants chirped madly. Melanie's tingling laughter drifted up towards them as she went into the pen to play with the little bundles of sunshine.

Upstairs in the loft, Tom rolled his eyes at Betty. Betty grinned in response.

Eventually Melanie tired of playing with the birds and returned to the house.

They watched on the computer screen as she made a cup of tea and then went into the bedroom.

"This is where you don't look," Betty said, angling the computer screen so it faced her and not Tom.

"Ah, why not," Tom joked. "I'm not recording yet."

Betty smirked and watched as Melanie climbed into bed and pulled a book out of her knapsack. She settled down to read, but quickly fell asleep sitting up in bed, the book open in her lap.

Betty saw movement on the side of the screen in the laneway and quickly moved the computer so that Tom could see it too. Tom immediately hit the record button. The cameras recorded directly onto the laptop.

Stew Mann biked into the yard on an old ten speed. He pulled up in front of the porch and leaned his bike against the railing. He started talking to someone or something off screen.

"Who the heck is he talking to," Tom hissed.

"No idea," Betty stammered.

They watched as Stew climbed the porch steps and opened the door. There was a blur as an enormous creature raced up the steps, knocked him down and continued into the house.

"Oh, no, it's Gertrude," Betty gasped.

"Figures," Tom blurted out.

"She's not supposed to be able to get up to the house," Betty fumed, defending her pig.

Betty watched in horror as Gertrude barreled through the house and into the bedroom where a startled Melanie sat bolt upright in bed, the pig's snout inches from her face.

They didn't need the audio in the house to hear Melanie's screams, they could hear her just fine out in the barn.

Stew stumbled to his feet and raced into the house to scoot the pig out of the bedroom.

"What are you doing here," Melanie yelled from the far corner of the bed where she huddled in fear.

"Oh, man, it's over," Betty wailed. "I may as well go down and retrieve Gertie."

"Not yet," Tom stopped her, "looks like the fun is just getting started. Look!"

Betty looked at the screen. A Jeep Cherokee drove up to the

house and Gwen Mann got out. She reached into the back seat and pulled out a shotgun.

"Oh, Good Lord," Betty quipped. "We have to stop this Tom."

"Yeah, we do, but I'm going in first."

Betty nodded as they both ran to the stairs. They climbed down the ladder's rungs and then bolted across the yard to the house.

On the computer screen, the camera followed Gwen into the house; the shotgun loaded and ready to bear. She stormed through the kitchen and into the bedroom, raising the shotgun and pulling both triggers back on the double barrel as she did so. She leveled it at her husband.

"Gwen, stop," Betty screamed as she ran across the path to the house, arms pumping, Tom Powder drawing his weapon as he matched her pace.

Gertrude heard Betty's voice and barged past Stew. She knocked Gwen aside in the process. Gwen stumbled, her fingers automatically closing in on the twin triggers of the shotgun. There was a loud click as the triggers hit the small circle of gunpowder, setting off the charge.

Kaboom!

The shotgun went off.

***

The Persephone was moored in the bay to the southeast of the McDonald's acreage and farm. A quarter moon hung in the sky, floating over the water as if it was God's puppet. The Milky Way glittered overhead.

Frank and Rainbow slept on an air mattress on deck, the two dogs curled up on blankets beside them.

Vi and Archie had gone to sleep below.

Restless, Reggie sat with his feet up on the bridge. Until the night was over, sleep was something he wouldn't be getting any of.

He worried about Betty even though Tom Powder seemed a capable fellow and he had promised him he wouldn't let Betty put herself into any direct danger. Reggie knew that life had a way of interfering with one's plans.

A woman's scream echoed across the water.

The dogs leapt to their feet. Champ growled. The Heeler bayed like a hound dog.

"What was that?" Archie bellowed from below deck.

"Was that a woman's scream," Rainbow cried, waking her husband from his deep slumber.

"It was," Reggie muttered, slipping quickly out of the pilot-house. He strode across the deck to the dingy tied to the back of the trawler. He pulled the mooring line hand over hand until the fiberglass dingy banged against the side of the hull.

Kaboom!

A shotgun blast rang through the night.

"I'm going in, you folks stay here where it's safe," he growled.

"Not without me," Frank insisted.

"Or me," Archie added, now wide awake.

Vi joined the others on deck.

"Now, wait just a minute, you two, I don't think Bets would like me putting you guys in danger like this," Reggie drawled.

"And every minute we stand here bickering, we're wasting time. My daughter could be dead for all I know," Archie glowered.

"You can't argue with him, Reggie," Vi stepped in. "Rainbow and I will stay here with the dogs unless you think Champ should go with you too."

"I'm good with that," Rainbow agreed.

"No, he's better staying here," Reggie grumbled. "We don't know what happened. Ya may need him."

Reggie climbed into the dingy and then helped Frank and Archie down too. The two men sat down. He placed the oars in the holders and put his back into it.

Fear niggled at him. If he lost Betty because he wasn't there to protect her, he would never forgive himself.

***

Gertrude took Betty out at the knees. The repercussion from the shotgun blast rippled through the air. Betty slammed into Tom Powder. Tom's revolver sailed through the air as Tom flipped backwards over Betty. The gun bounced off Gertrude's head as she ran circles in the living room in a total panic.

"Gertie, stop," Betty squawked, gasping for air.

"You cheating scumbag," Gwen screamed at her husband as he laid writhing in pain on the floor, the top of his right arm singed black from the blast. Small round dots of blood appeared on his upper arm where the shotgun pellets had lodged in the muscle.

"Like you thought I didn't notice how much this girl looks like Tiffany," she continued to yell. "I kill her, now I kill you!"

"Oh, no you won't," Powder said, pushing himself to his knees. He scrambled forward after his pistol, which had slid under the coffee table in the living room.

Betty stood up. She put a hand to her head, the world tilting at a precarious angle. Her vision blurred, and she staggered forward, grabbing the wall for support.

Gertrude grunted and squealed. Her eyes were wide with fear.

"I got this, Betty, you look after getting Gert out of here," Tom ordered her too late.

Gwen flipped the shotgun over and clobbered Tom over the top of the head. He went down like a basketball in a hoop.

"Don't do it, Gwen," Betty mumbled as the world finally righted itself.

"What are you all doing here," the fearful bartender cried, the covers still tucked tightly up to her chin. Tears slid down her cheeks.

"I never slept with your husband, Gwen! Jeepers, he's old enough to be my father," Melanie cried.

"I don't believe you. He's a pig. He sleeps with anything," Gwen yelled.

"Well, not with me," the young woman countered.

"She's right, Gwen, I haven't slept with her," Stew whispered, his face twisted with pain.

"Then what are you doing here at two in the morning," she hollered at her husband.

"Melanie forgot her wallet at the bar," he said, writhing on the floor. "I was going to leave it on the kitchen table and go home."

"And you just confessed to killing Tiffany, Gwen," Betty growled. "Did you kill Eliza too?"

Gwen lowered the shotgun.

Betty seized the opportunity and staggered forward. She grabbed the barrel of the shotgun and yanked backwards with all her might. Gwen slammed into her like a bumper car. They fell, one on top of the other.

"Let go! I want to shoot him anyway," Gwen yelled hysterically. "He cheated on me our whole marriage. I don't believe him. I don't believe anything he says."

"Then believe me," Melanie sobbed. "I'd never cheat with a married man, no matter who they were."

Gwen let go of the shotgun. She rolled over and looked Melanie in the eye.

Betty grabbed the shotgun from out of Gwen's lap.

Tom moaned. His eyes flickered open.

"I'd never do that to you," Melanie said to Gwen.

Gwen crumbled. Tears flowed copiously from her eyes. It was like the Heaven's Gate had opened. She sobbed uncontrollably.

Gertrude, sensing that the worst was over, clip-clopped on cloven hooves across the oak floor and over to the two women sitting on the living room floor outside of the bedroom's door. She stepped over Tom's semi-conscious form.

"I can't believe you killed Tiffany," Stew mumbled, propping himself up against the bed.

"You were going to leave me. I couldn't let you do that," Gwen stuttered. "Who would look after my mother and father, eh? We have pre-nup, remember?"

"Jeez, Gwen, I wouldn't have left you with nothing," Stew confessed. "You doubled business since we got married and you took over managing the day-to-day operations of the pub. I loved Tiffany. If she'd have had me, yes, I would have asked you for a divorce, but far as I'm concerned, you're a fifty-fifty partner in the pub. That wouldn't have changed, and I figured you'd be glad to get rid of me."

Gwen sobbed.

Reggie, Frank and Archie flew into the little one-bedroom house.

"Bets, are you all right," Reggie yelled, rushing to her side.

Frank ran over to help Tom sit up.

"Gertie, come on, let's get you out of here," Archie cajoled the pot-bellied pig.

"I'm fine, honey," Betty replied, "just help me up."

Reggie helped Betty to her feet as Frank helped Tom sit up. Tom pulled out his handcuffs and handed them to Betty.

"Gwen Mann," Betty said, slipping the handcuffs around the tiny pub owner's wrists, "you have the right to remain silent. Anything you say can and will be used against you in a court of law…"

After Betty finished reading Gwen her rights, she removed Gwen from the living room and sat her down at the kitchen table.

"Dad, Reggie, watch her, will you," she asked the two men.

They both nodded in agreement.

"I got this," Frank told her as she walked past him and Tom. Tom held his head in his hands, still recovering from the whack on the head.

Betty bent to examine Stew's shoulder.

"You'll live," she advised him. "It's gonna hurt, but it's a good thing that gun was loaded with buckshot."

"I'm so sorry," Stew sniffled.

"For what, Stew," she asked sarcastically.

"Yeah, for what," Melanie echoed. "And if you were just dropping off my wallet, why were you in the bedroom when Gwen showed up?"

"I think I need am ambulance," he stuttered helplessly, unable to face either woman.

"And a new bartender," Melanie spat at him.

Betty sighed and yanked out her cell phone. She bypassed 911 and phoned Tom's office instead, requesting to speak directly to the Desk Sergeant in charge of the night shift.

The Fat Lady Sings

Flood lights stood on stacks of firewood, illuminating a make-shift helicopter pad in the middle of Frank and Rainbow's meadow as the sun peeked over the eastern horizon and the quarter moon sank below the earth's axis.

The medical evacuation helicopter had just left with Tom and Stew on board. The blow to Tom's head proved more serious than Stew's peppering with buckshot.

Ben Hammerton strode back and forth between the helicopter pad and the house while a dozen officers bustled back and forth from the barn to the house to the police boat anchored offshore.

Hammerton had quickly organized it all after the Desk Sergeant had called him at home and filled him in on the situation. He had flown in by police helicopter with a paramedic on board to assess the situation.

"Why the Hell were you guys doing this alone without back-up," he barked at Betty.

"Because Tom and I weren't sure that this would work," Betty growled back.

"It was a lame brain scheme that could have got you both killed," he yelled, "not to mention the fact that you put an innocent civilian in danger. That Melanie girl could have been killed."

"Hey, we were right there monitoring and recording everything and since Gwen poisoned Tiffany, I never thought she'd have the guts to use a gun."

"'Never thought' are the keywords, Special Agent," he grumbled.

The two stood facing off, hands on hips. Reggie, Frank and Archie sipped coffee on the porch, watching the fireworks.

Rainbow, Melanie and Vi joined the men, mugs of tea in hand.

"Now that the sun is rising, you can see that the thyme, sage and heather are all starting to flower. I'm already getting ready to pick some mint. The Echinacea won't be ready until the summer and the wild roses still have to bloom before I can pick the rosehips," Rainbow said animatedly.

"I can't wait for you to start packaging and selling herbs and teas again," Vi gushed. "Rainbow would be so thrilled."

"Yes, her spirit is at rest," Rainbow assured them.

"I'd love to work for you," Melanie gushed. "This is more what I'm into than bartending. I don't mind pitching a tent or sleeping in the barn until I can find some place to stay on the island."

"I sure don't mind," Frank agreed. "We'll rig something up for you. What do you think, babe?"

"That'd be great. We can't pay a lot until we get going though," Rainbow said worriedly.

"S'okay, I'll work on commission to start. We can get a booth at some farmer's markets."

"Talk to me afore you goes and puts money down fer rent, Mel," Reggie said. "Bets and I have to figure some things out, and we got two houses and a boat between us. Ya can stay on *The Persephone* in the meantime."

"Oh, that's sweet of you, Reggie," Melanie replied, her eyes as bright as a puppy's.

"Maybe you should let her stay in your cabin, Reggie," Vi beamed. "I hear there are a few nice young bachelors working in your greenhouses."

"Yes'um there is that," he replied over the rim of his coffee cup.

Betty finally gave up arguing with Ben Hammerton and stalked away, leaving the young detective standing with his hands in the air in supplication.

Archie, Vi, and Reggie chuckled. They knew that if the detective thought he would get the last word in with Betty, he would be sorely disappointed.

"So what now, Angel puss," her father asked her.

"Gwen's on the boat. She's being charged with first degree murder and attempted murder," Betty said breathlessly.

"So we can put two murders to bed," her father stammered.

"We can," Betty agreed.

"But neither Gwen nor Camille said that they killed my sister-in-law," Vi exclaimed.

"No, they didn't," Betty said, her heart breaking for not being able to solve all of her friend's deaths.

"Well, two out of three isn't bad, is it," Frank asked innocently.

Rainbow swatted him on the arm.

"No, it's not all that bad, Frank," Betty grinned, despite herself.

Reggie stood up and walked over to wrap his arms around the love of his life. Betty leaned into his broad chest.

"You know, Angel, I was there that morning that Eliza died," Archie trembled. "I know now I should have told you sooner. However bizarre it was, I think Eliza's death was an accident."

"She never did well with heights," Vi added. "Even step stools used to make her get dizzy, she told me once."

"Ya knows," Reggie said, "Eliza had a pretty strange sense of humor."

"That she did," Archie chuckled.

"You think drowning in her fish tank was fitting," Betty gasped, horrified.

"I do, and she was my sister-in-law," Vi chortled. "I think she'd find it hilarious."

"Probably proud of herself," Archie mumbled.

Vi swatted his arm.

Reggie let out a lengthy sigh of relief.

Betty looked from Reggie to her father and then at Vi, stupefied.

"I think I'll head over to the barn now that the helicopter's gone and let the dogs out," Frank said, breaking the tension.

"Don't let Gert or Peaches out," Archie grumbled. "They'll probably go bowling for cops."

"Father," Betty exclaimed.

As one, the group burst into a round of laughter.

"I'm coming with," Rainbow chirruped.

"Me too," Melanie said.

"I think we all will," Vi finished.

As one, the friends and extended family strode arm in arm past the gurgling pond and small waterfall that stood where the stone angel used to be. They gamboled past the flowering herbs and early roses, towards the barn to release the hounds and possibly one very naughty pot-bellied pig and her bestie, a Jersey cow named Peaches.

And then the pig got loose…

The End… or is it?

Want more? Keep reading…
Book Four in The Gumboot & Gumshoe Series, Gertrude & The Sorcerer's Gold
is now available.

If you enjoyed this novel, and all the rest of the series, please consider leaving an honest review or by rating it on Amazon, Bookbub, or Goodreads. Why leave a review? Reviews help readers find books and discover amazing new stories. It only takes a minute of your time to leave a review and it means a lot to the author and their publishing company.

For more information on Laura Hesse, or to learn about upcoming releases, go to:

www.RunningLProductions.com

Novels by Laura Hesse

The Holiday Series:

One Frosty Christmas, The Great Pumpkin Ride,

A Filly Called Easter, Independence, and *Valentino*

The Gumboot & Gumshoe Series:

Book One: *Gumboots, Gumshoes & Murder*

Book Two: *The Dastardly Mr. Deeds*

Book Three: *Murder Most Fowl.*

Book Four: *Gertrude & The Sorcerer's Gold*

The Silver Spurs Series:

The Silver Spurs Home for Aging Cowgirls

Bandits, Broads & Dirty Dawgs

Who Killed Cade

Paranormal Romance

Lucifer and Mary Jane: Who Stole the Devil's Horses

Learn more at www.RunningLProductions.com